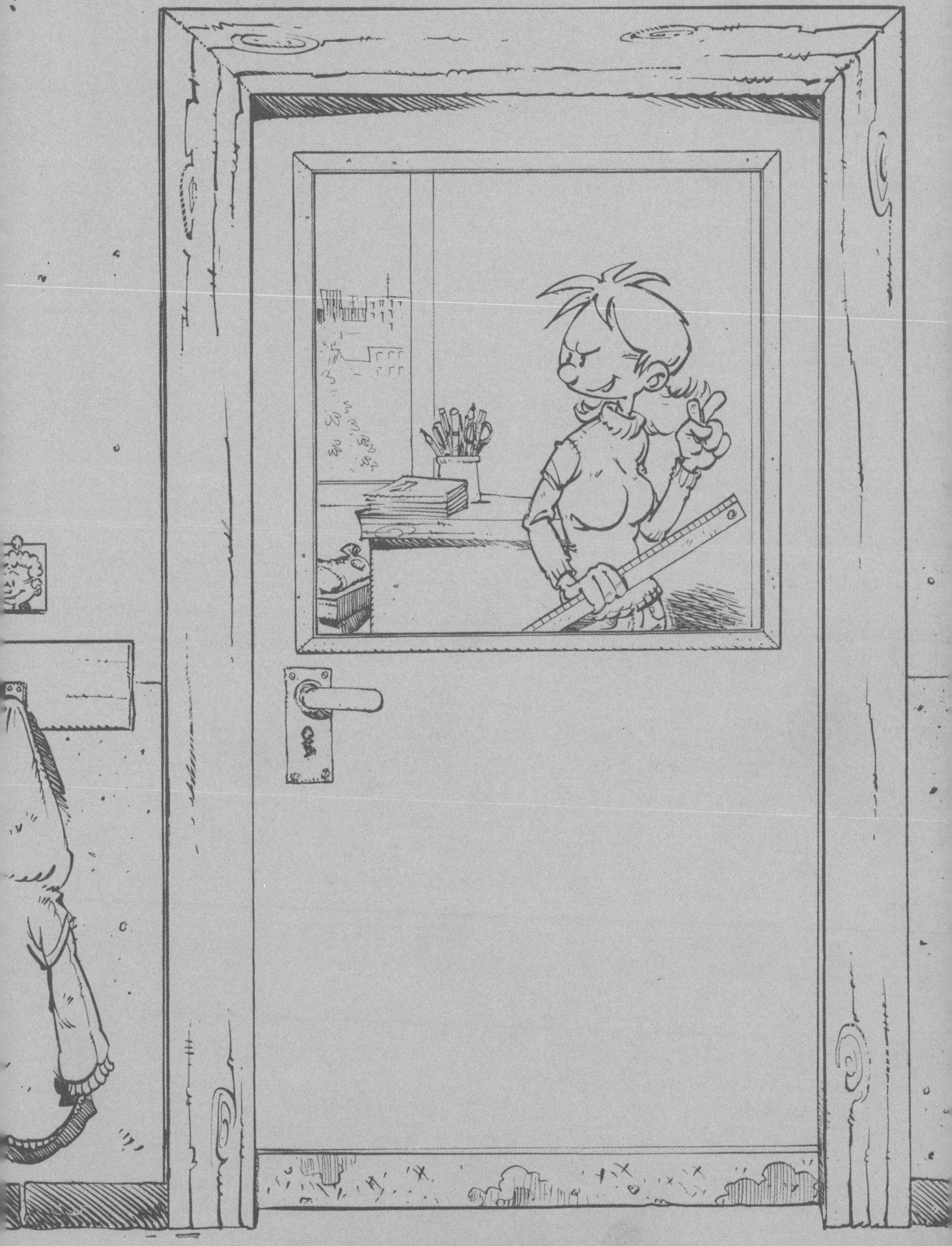

toto
TROUBLE

Thierry Coppée • Story and Art
Lorien • Color

PAPERCUTZ™
New York

Thanks to Valérie, Théo and Julien for their
patience and support.
Thanks to Mich for his February message.
Thanks to Guy for his trust.
Thanks to Lorien for listening.
Thanks to Thierry for his work behind the scenes.

To my parents and grandparents.

TOTO TROUBLE Graphic Novels
Available from Papercutz

Graphic Novel #1
"Back to Crass"

Coming Soon!
Graphic Novel #2
"A Deadly Jokester"

TOTO TROUBLE graphic novels are available for $7.99 in paperback, and $12.99 in hardcover. Available from booksellers everywhere. You can also order online from papercutz.com. Or call 1-800-886-1223, Monday through Friday, 9 – 5 EST. MC, Visa, and AmEx accepted. To order by mail, please add $4.00 for postage and handling for first book ordered, $1.00 for each additional book, and make check payable to NBM Publishing. Send to: Papercutz, 160 Broadway, Suite 700, East Wing, New York, NY 10038.

papercutz.com

TOTO TROUBLE #1 "Back to Crass"
Les Blagues de Toto, volumes 1-2, Coppée
© Éditions Delcourt, 2003-2004

Thierry Coppée – Writer & Artist
Lorien – Colorist
Joe Johnson – Translation
Tom Orzechowski – Lettering
Michael Petranek – Associate Editor
Jim Salicrup
Editor-in-Chief

ISBN: 978-1-59707-726-2 paperback edition
ISBN: 978-1-59707-777-4 hardcover edition

Printed in China
April 2014 by New Era Printing LTD
Unit C, 8/F, Worldwide Centre
123 Tung Chau Street, Hong Kong

Papercutz books may be purchased for business or promotional use.
For information on bulk purchases please contact Macmillan Corporate and
Premium Sales Department at (800) 221-7945 x5442.

Distributed by Macmillan
First Papercutz Printing

"My Name is Toto"

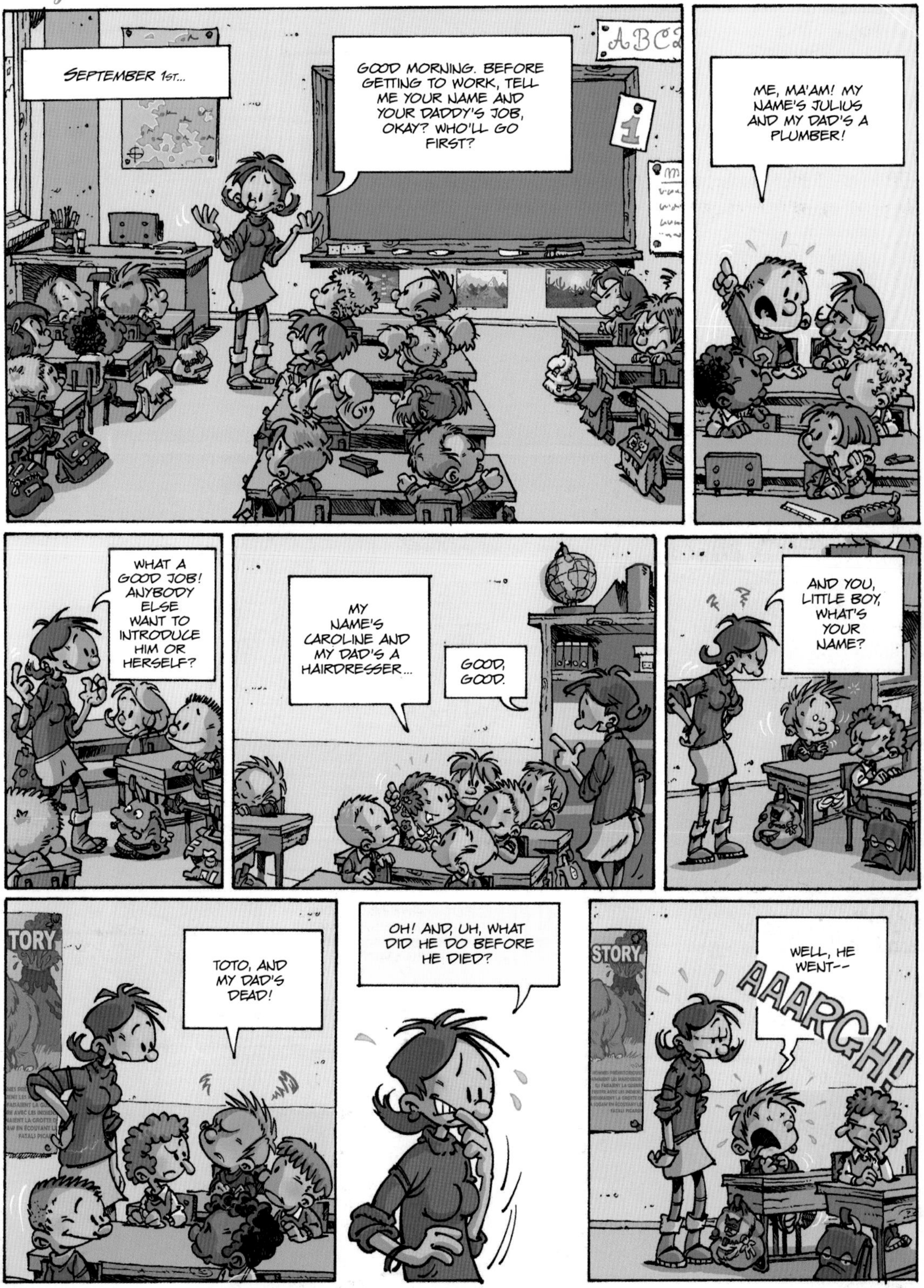
SEPTEMBER 1ST...
GOOD MORNING. BEFORE GETTING TO WORK, TELL ME YOUR NAME AND YOUR DADDY'S JOB, OKAY? WHO'LL GO FIRST?
ME, MA'AM! MY NAME'S JULIUS AND MY DAD'S A PLUMBER!
WHAT A GOOD JOB! ANYBODY ELSE WANT TO INTRODUCE HIM OR HERSELF?
MY NAME'S CAROLINE AND MY DAD'S A HAIRDRESSER...
GOOD, GOOD.
AND YOU, LITTLE BOY, WHAT'S YOUR NAME?
TOTO, AND MY DAD'S DEAD!
OH! AND, UH, WHAT DID HE DO BEFORE HE DIED?
WELL, HE WENT--
AAARGH!

"Thinking of You..."

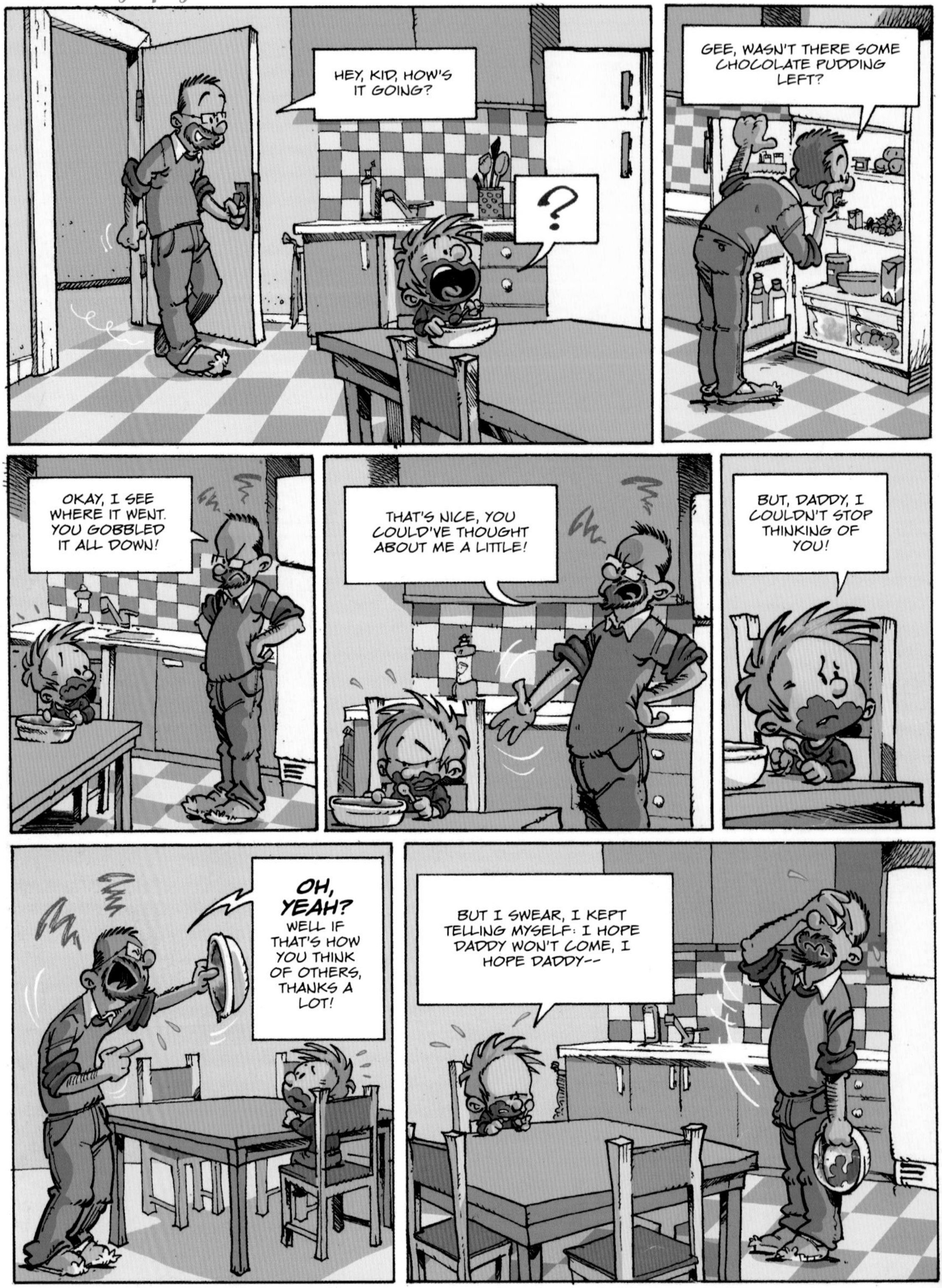
HEY, KID, HOW'S IT GOING?
?
GEE, WASN'T THERE SOME CHOCOLATE PUDDING LEFT?
OKAY, I SEE WHERE IT WENT. YOU GOBBLED IT ALL DOWN!
THAT'S NICE, YOU COULD'VE THOUGHT ABOUT ME A LITTLE!
BUT, DADDY, I COULDN'T STOP THINKING OF YOU!
OH, YEAH? WELL IF THAT'S HOW YOU THINK OF OTHERS, THANKS A LOT!
BUT I SWEAR, I KEPT TELLING MYSELF: I HOPE DADDY WON'T COME, I HOPE DADDY--

"Questions for a Champion-1"

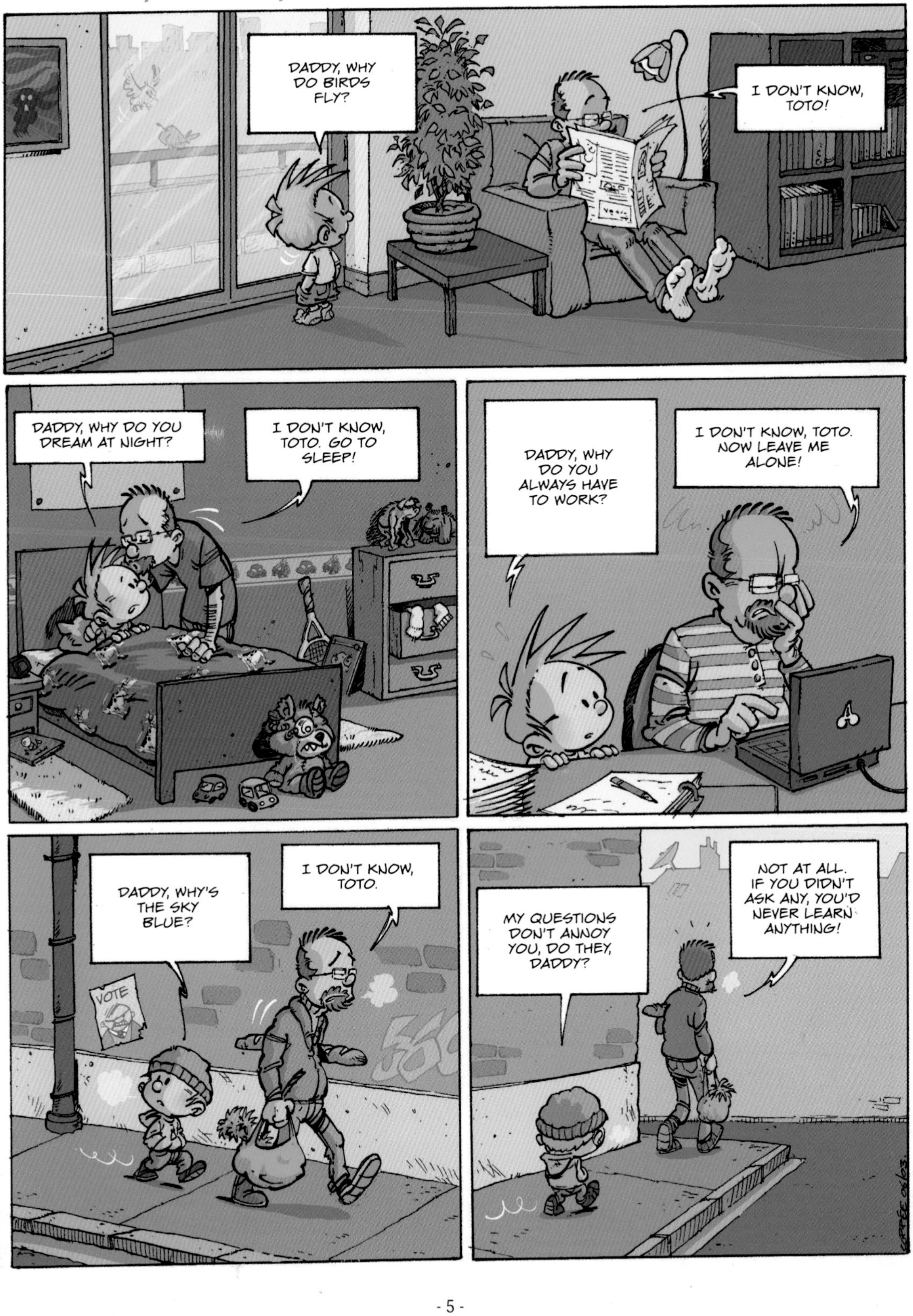
DADDY, WHY DO BIRDS FLY?
I DON'T KNOW, TOTO!
DADDY, WHY DO YOU DREAM AT NIGHT?
I DON'T KNOW, TOTO. GO TO SLEEP!
DADDY, WHY DO YOU ALWAYS HAVE TO WORK?
I DON'T KNOW, TOTO. NOW LEAVE ME ALONE!
DADDY, WHY'S THE SKY BLUE?
I DON'T KNOW, TOTO.
VOTE
MY QUESTIONS DON'T ANNOY YOU, DO THEY, DADDY?
NOT AT ALL. IF YOU DIDN'T ASK ANY, YOU'D NEVER LEARN ANYTHING!

"I Love You, But..."

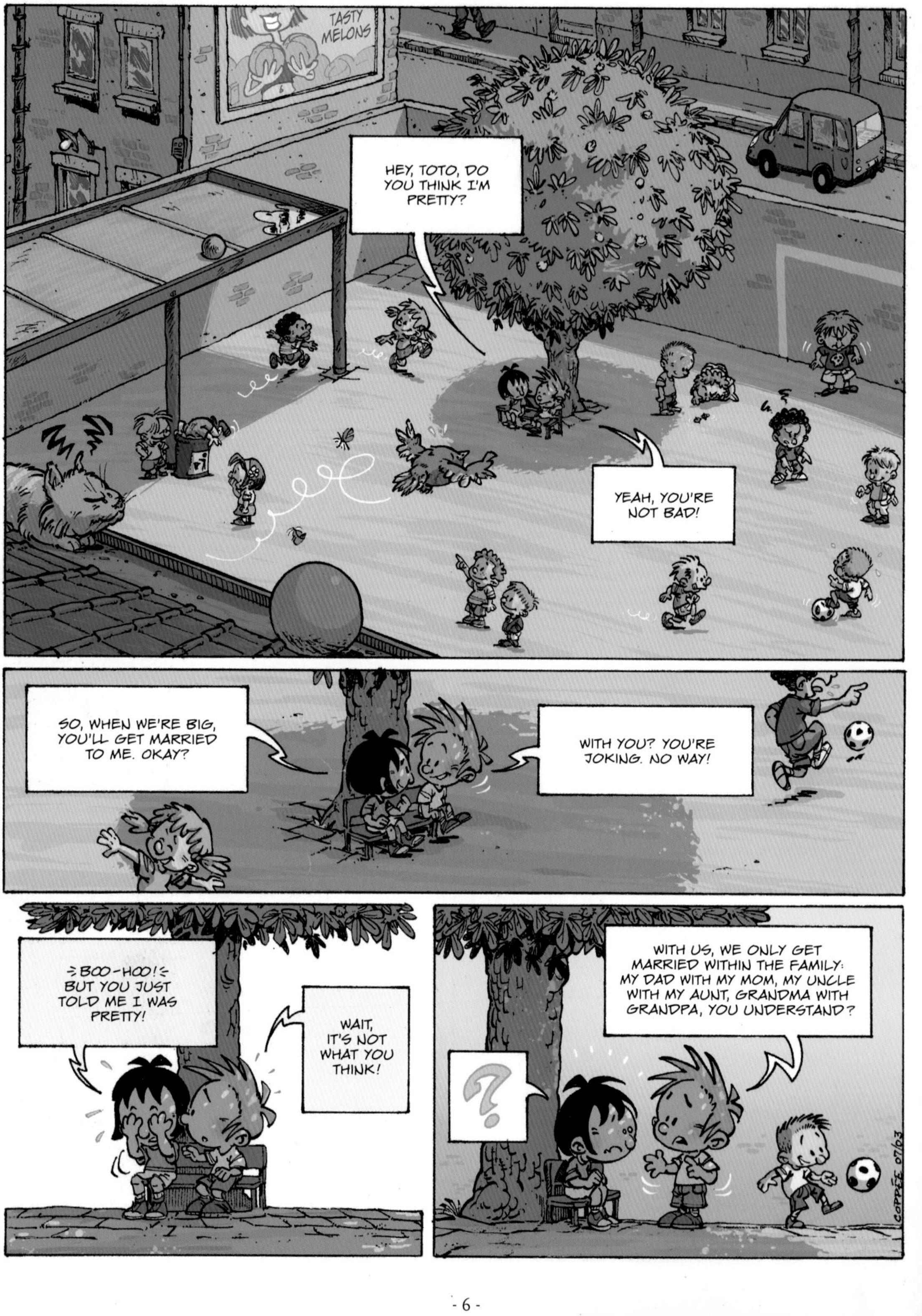

TASTY MELONS
HEY, TOTO, DO YOU THINK I'M PRETTY?
YEAH, YOU'RE NOT BAD!
SO, WHEN WE'RE BIG, YOU'LL GET MARRIED TO ME. OKAY?
WITH YOU? YOU'RE JOKING. NO WAY!
BOO-HOO! BUT YOU JUST TOLD ME I WAS PRETTY!
WAIT, IT'S NOT WHAT YOU THINK!
WITH US, WE ONLY GET MARRIED WITHIN THE FAMILY: MY DAD WITH MY MOM, MY UNCLE WITH MY AUNT, GRANDMA WITH GRANDPA, YOU UNDERSTAND?
?
COPPÉE 07/03

"*Hamming It Up*"

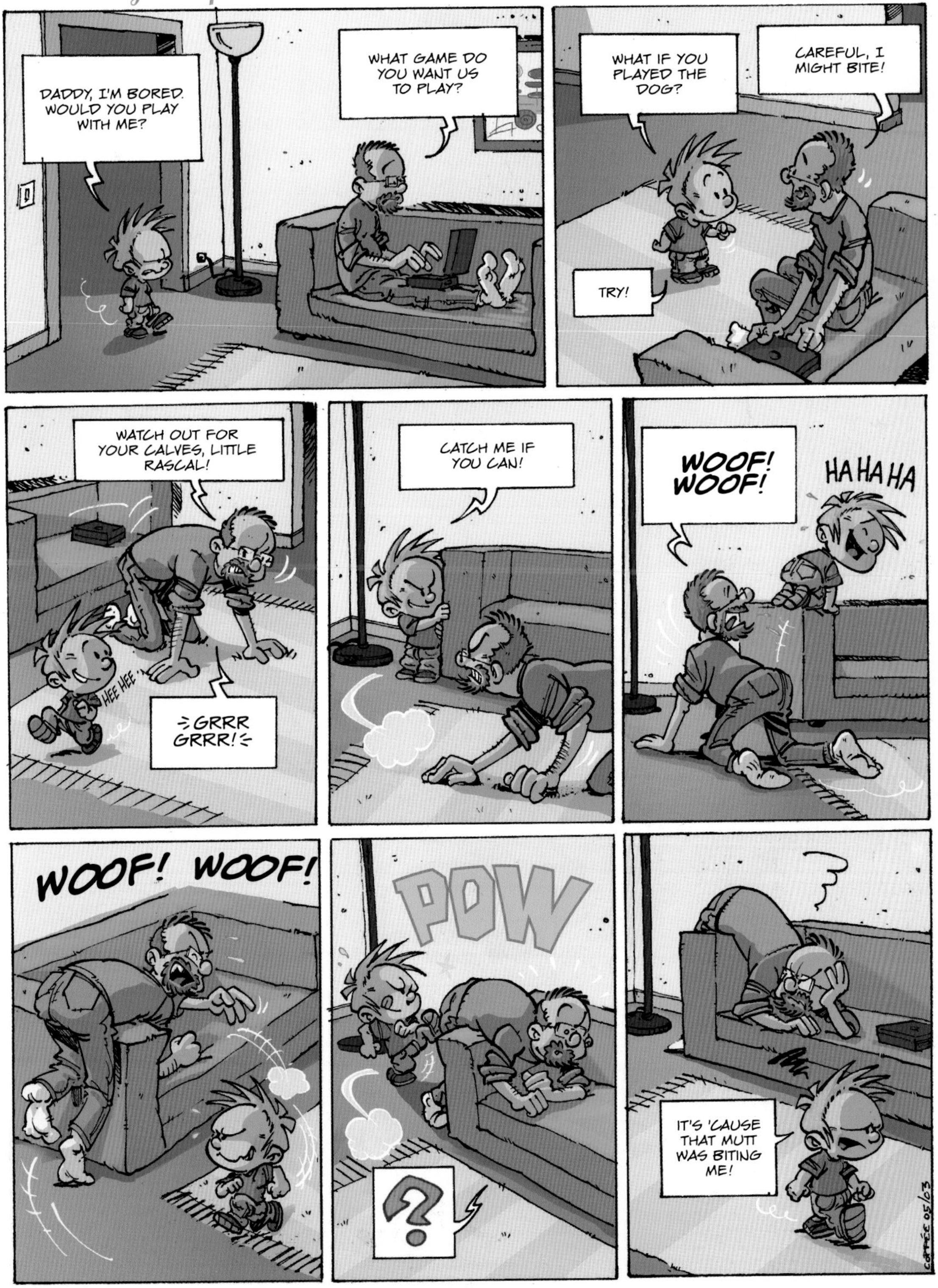
DADDY, I'M BORED. WOULD YOU PLAY WITH ME?
WHAT GAME DO YOU WANT US TO PLAY?
WHAT IF YOU PLAYED THE DOG?
CAREFUL, I MIGHT BITE!
TRY!
WATCH OUT FOR YOUR CALVES, LITTLE RASCAL!
HEE HEE
GRRR GRRR!
CATCH ME IF YOU CAN!
WOOF! WOOF!
HA HA HA
WOOF! WOOF!
POW
?
IT'S 'CAUSE THAT MUTT WAS BITING ME!
COPPÉE 05/03

"A Big Head"

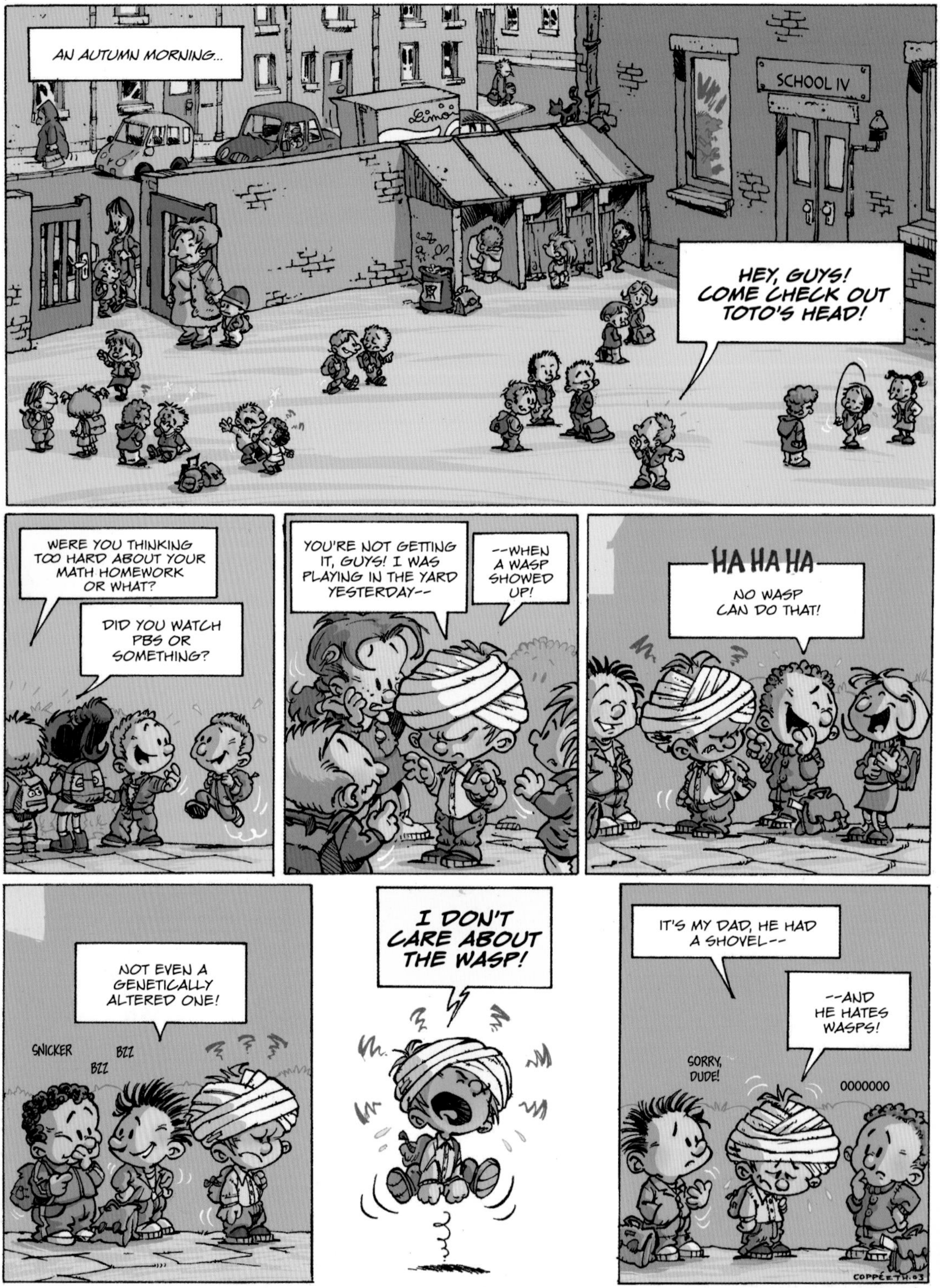
AN AUTUMN MORNING...
SCHOOL IV
HEY, GUYS! COME CHECK OUT TOTO'S HEAD!
WERE YOU THINKING TOO HARD ABOUT YOUR MATH HOMEWORK OR WHAT?
DID YOU WATCH PBS OR SOMETHING?
YOU'RE NOT GETTING IT, GUYS! I WAS PLAYING IN THE YARD YESTERDAY--
--WHEN A WASP SHOWED UP!
HA HA HA
NO WASP CAN DO THAT!
NOT EVEN A GENETICALLY ALTERED ONE!
SNICKER
BZZ
BZZ
I DON'T CARE ABOUT THE WASP!
IT'S MY DAD, HE HAD A SHOVEL--
--AND HE HATES WASPS!
SORRY, DUDE!
OOOOOOO
COPPÉE TH.03

"The Coffin"

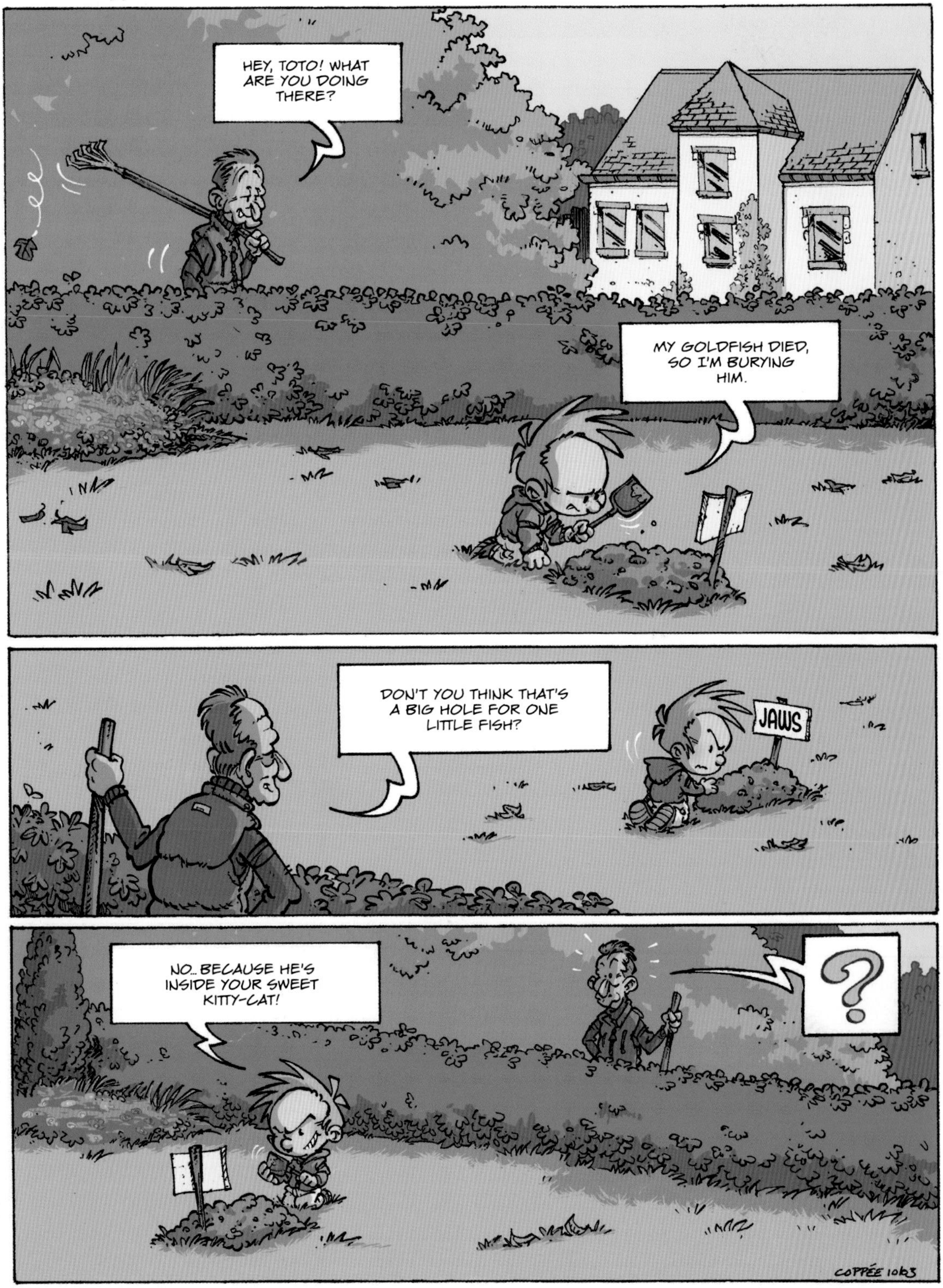
HEY, TOTO! WHAT ARE YOU DOING THERE?
MY GOLDFISH DIED, SO I'M BURYING HIM.
DON'T YOU THINK THAT'S A BIG HOLE FOR ONE LITTLE FISH?
JAWS
NO... BECAUSE HE'S INSIDE YOUR SWEET KITTY-CAT!
?
COPPÉE 10/03

"Singing the Times Table"

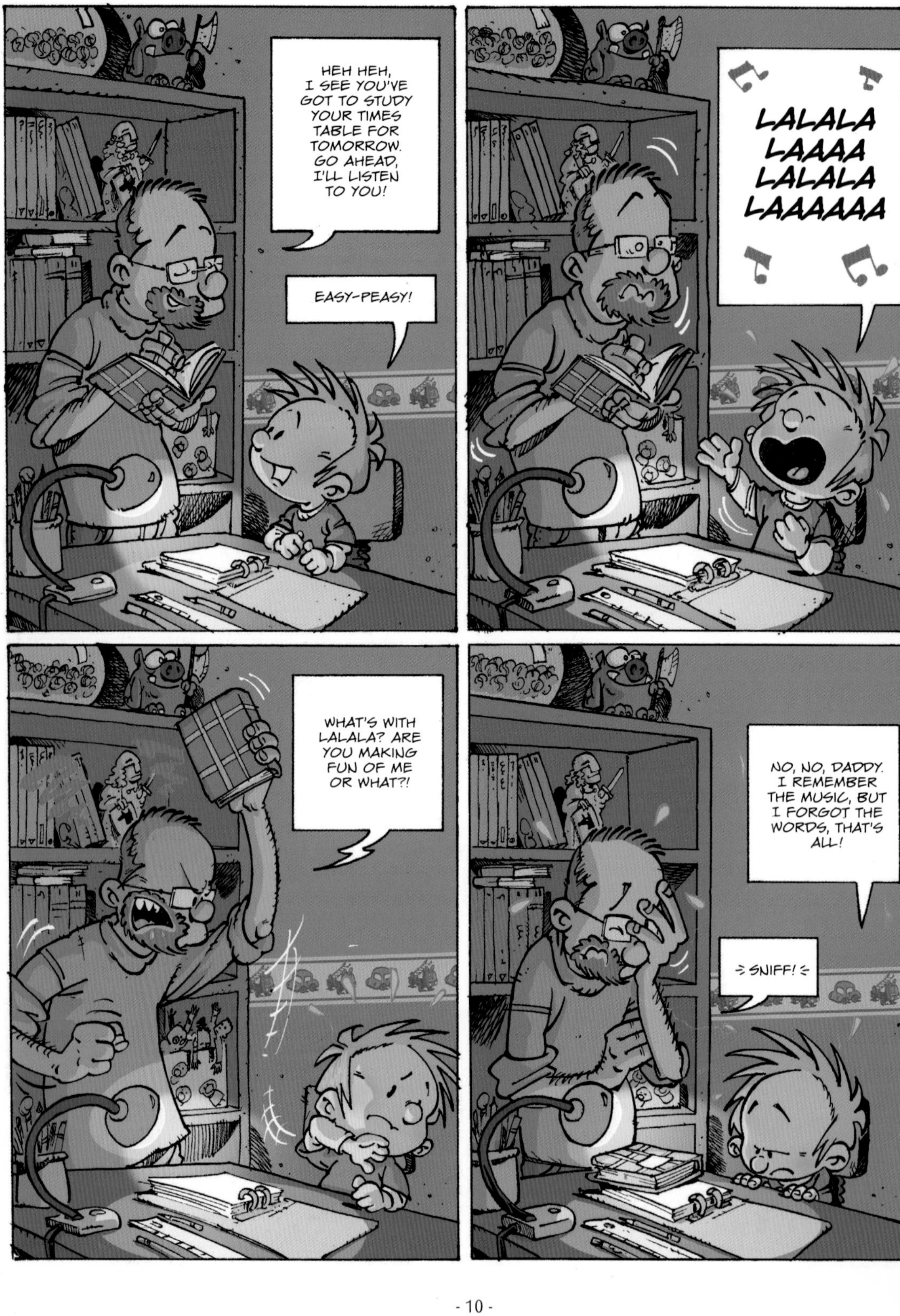
HEH HEH, I SEE YOU'VE GOT TO STUDY YOUR TIMES TABLE FOR TOMORROW. GO AHEAD, I'LL LISTEN TO YOU!
EASY-PEASY!
LALALA LAAAA LALALA LAAAAAA
WHAT'S WITH LALALA? ARE YOU MAKING FUN OF ME OR WHAT?!
NO, NO, DADDY. I REMEMBER THE MUSIC, BUT I FORGOT THE WORDS, THAT'S ALL!
SNIFF!

"After School"

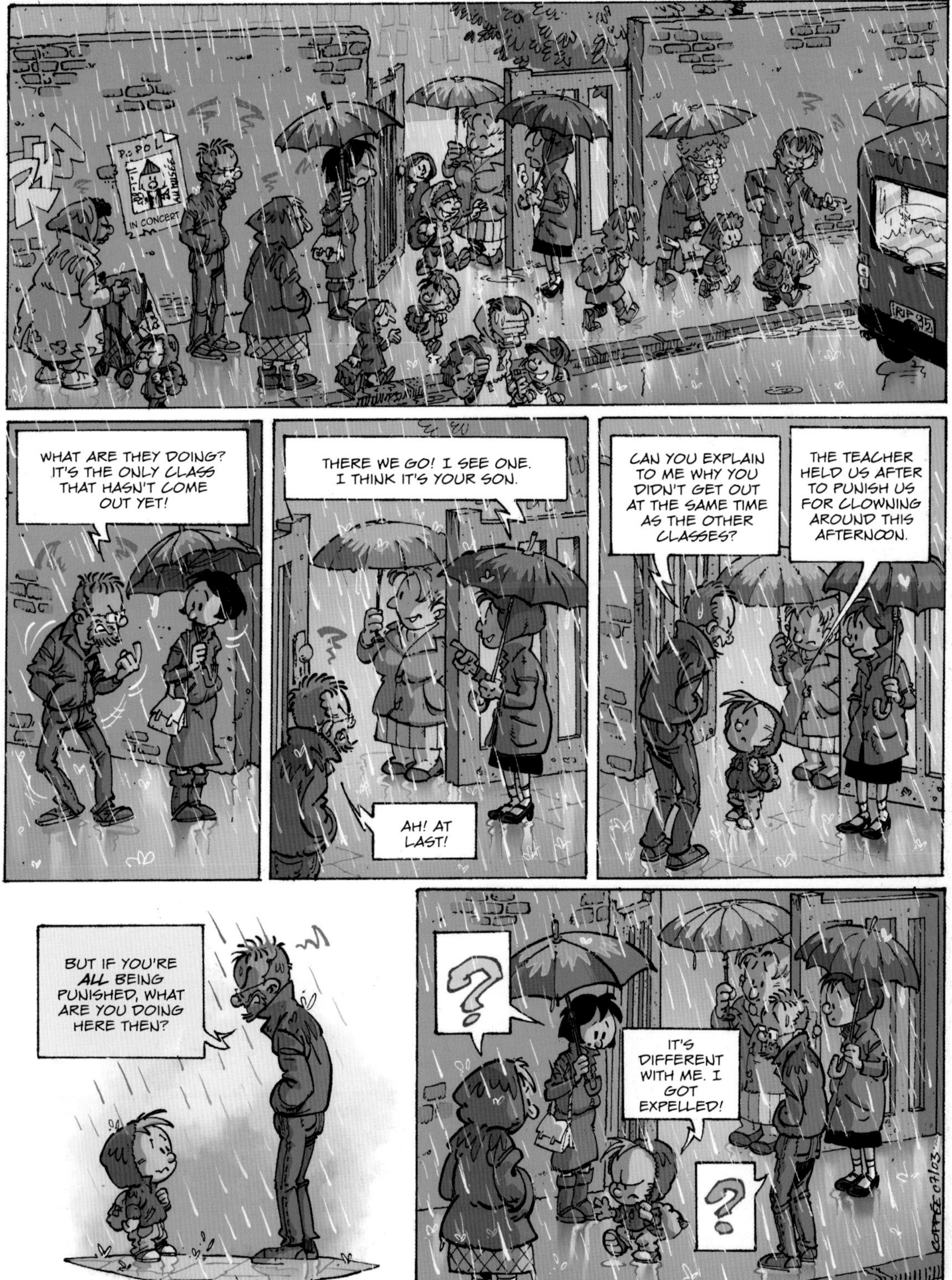
IN CONCERT
WHAT ARE THEY DOING? IT'S THE ONLY CLASS THAT HASN'T COME OUT YET!
THERE WE GO! I SEE ONE. I THINK IT'S YOUR SON.
AH! AT LAST!
CAN YOU EXPLAIN TO ME WHY YOU DIDN'T GET OUT AT THE SAME TIME AS THE OTHER CLASSES?
THE TEACHER HELD US AFTER TO PUNISH US FOR CLOWNING AROUND THIS AFTERNOON.
BUT IF YOU'RE ALL BEING PUNISHED, WHAT ARE YOU DOING HERE THEN?
?
IT'S DIFFERENT WITH ME. I GOT EXPELLED!
?

"Chew Your Food"

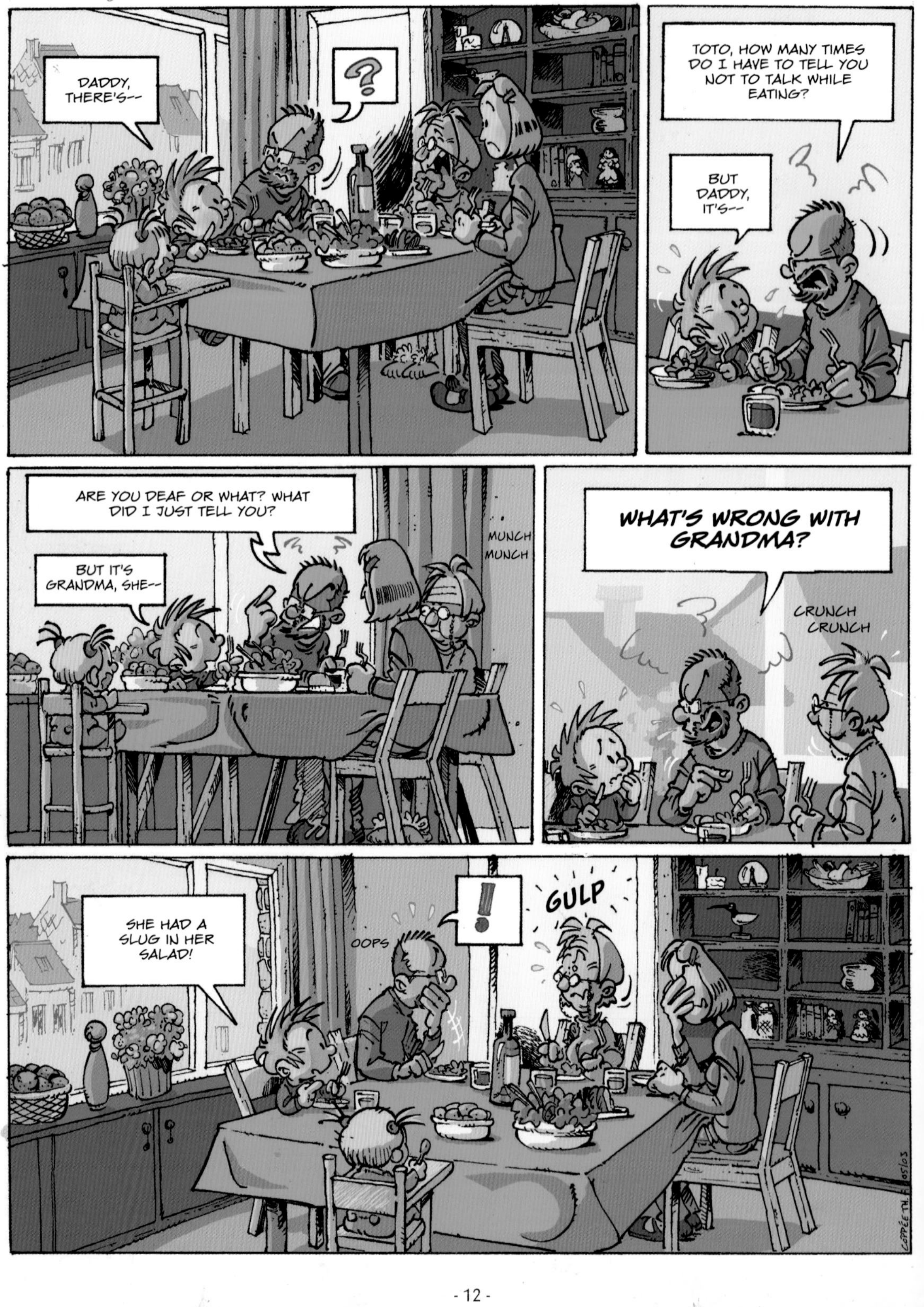
DADDY, THERE'S--
?
TOTO, HOW MANY TIMES DO I HAVE TO TELL YOU NOT TO TALK WHILE EATING?
BUT DADDY, IT'S--
ARE YOU DEAF OR WHAT? WHAT DID I JUST TELL YOU?
BUT IT'S GRANDMA, SHE--
MUNCH MUNCH
WHAT'S WRONG WITH GRANDMA?
CRUNCH CRUNCH
SHE HAD A SLUG IN HER SALAD!
OOPS
!
GULP

"The Puzzle Genius"

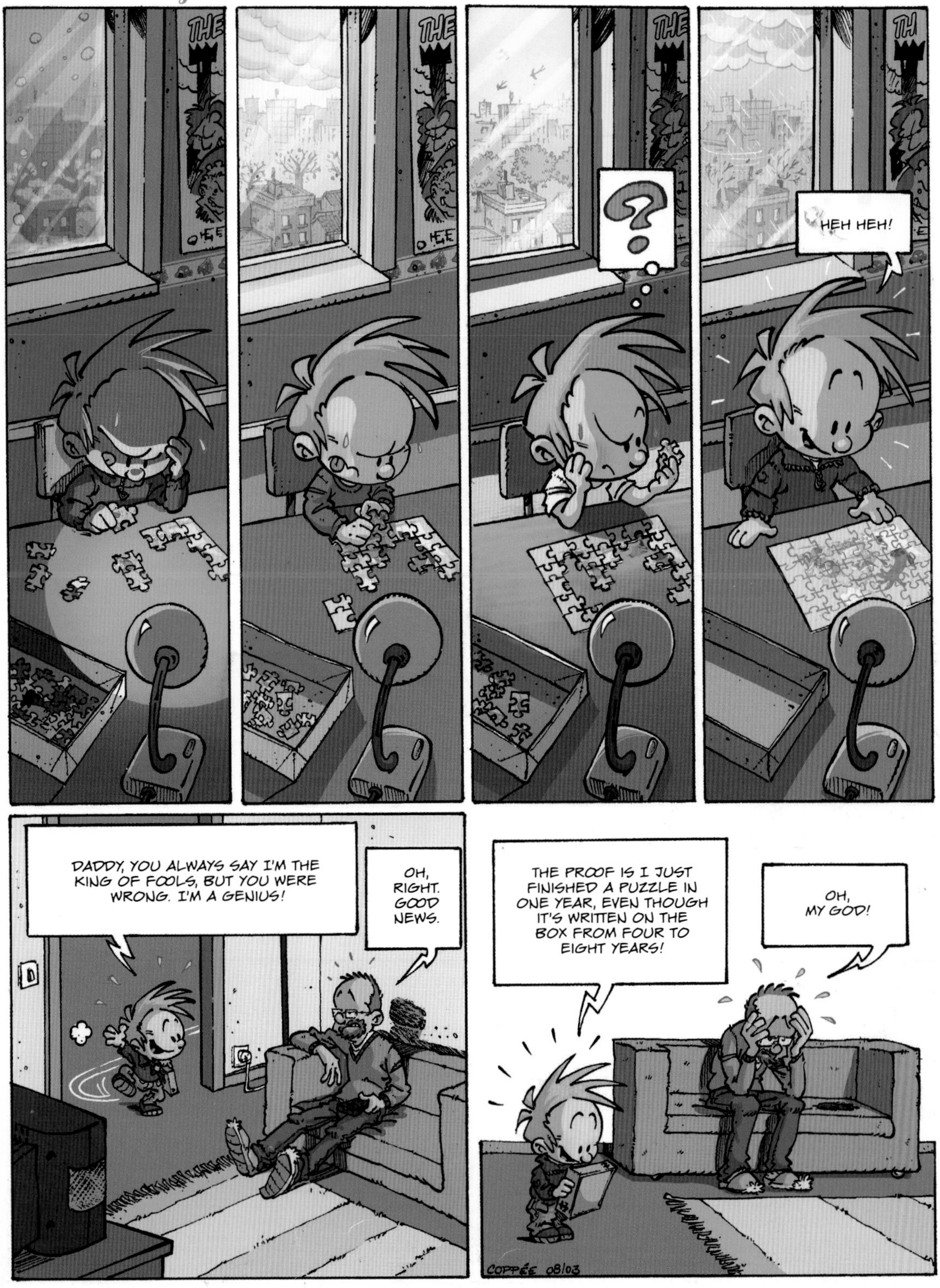
HEH HEH!
DADDY, YOU ALWAYS SAY I'M THE KING OF FOOLS, BUT YOU WERE WRONG. I'M A GENIUS!
OH, RIGHT. GOOD NEWS.
THE PROOF IS I JUST FINISHED A PUZZLE IN ONE YEAR, EVEN THOUGH IT'S WRITTEN ON THE BOX FROM FOUR TO EIGHT YEARS!
OH, MY GOD!
COPPÉE 08/03

"The Good Idea"

MOMMY, CAN I SLEEP WITH YOU?

?

I SUSPECT YOU'RE TAKING ADVANTAGE OF DADDY BEING AWAY ON A BUSINESS TRIP TO COME IN HERE!

AM I WRONG?

PLEASE, MOMMY?

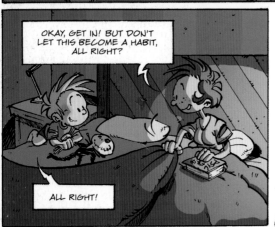

OKAY, GET IN! BUT DON'T LET THIS BECOME A HABIT, ALL RIGHT?

ALL RIGHT!

WANT TO PLAY DADDY AND MOMMY?

NO! WE'RE SLEEPING.

PLEASE?

FIVE MINUTES, THEN BEDDY-BYE!

COOL.

SAY, HONEY, I HAVE A GREAT IDEA FOR TOMORROW!

OH, YEAH?

I THOUGHT IT'D BE NICE IF WE GOT A MOUNTAIN BIKE FOR THE KID'S BIRTHDAY!

?

"Suggested Detergent"

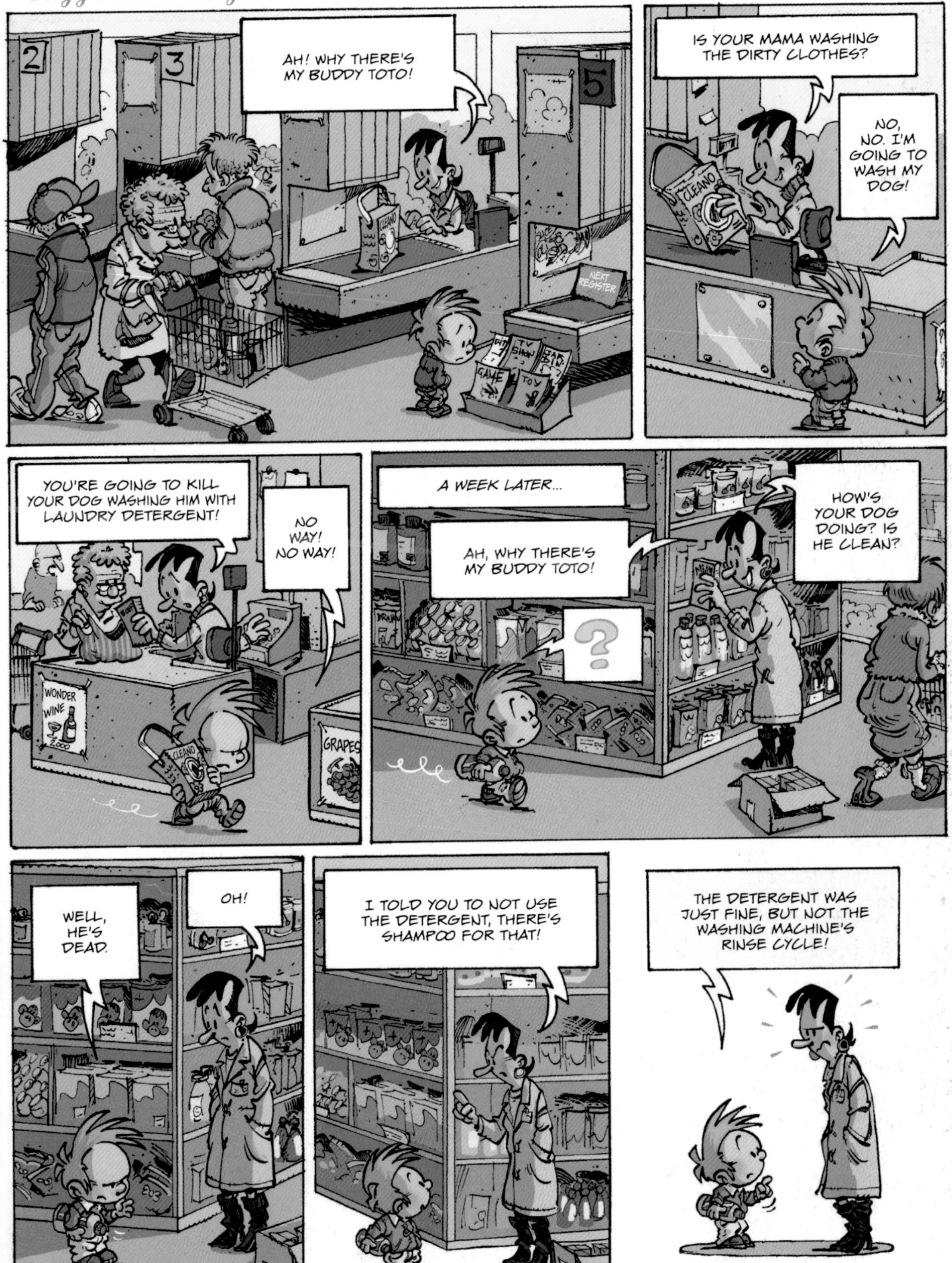

AH! WHY THERE'S MY BUDDY TOTO!
IS YOUR MAMA WASHING THE DIRTY CLOTHES?
NO, NO. I'M GOING TO WASH MY DOG!
YOU'RE GOING TO KILL YOUR DOG WASHING HIM WITH LAUNDRY DETERGENT!
NO WAY! NO WAY!
A WEEK LATER...
AH, WHY THERE'S MY BUDDY TOTO!
HOW'S YOUR DOG DOING? IS HE CLEAN?
?
WELL, HE'S DEAD.
OH!
I TOLD YOU TO NOT USE THE DETERGENT, THERE'S SHAMPOO FOR THAT!
THE DETERGENT WAS JUST FINE, BUT NOT THE WASHING MACHINE'S RINSE CYCLE!
COPPÉE 09/03

"The Martyr"

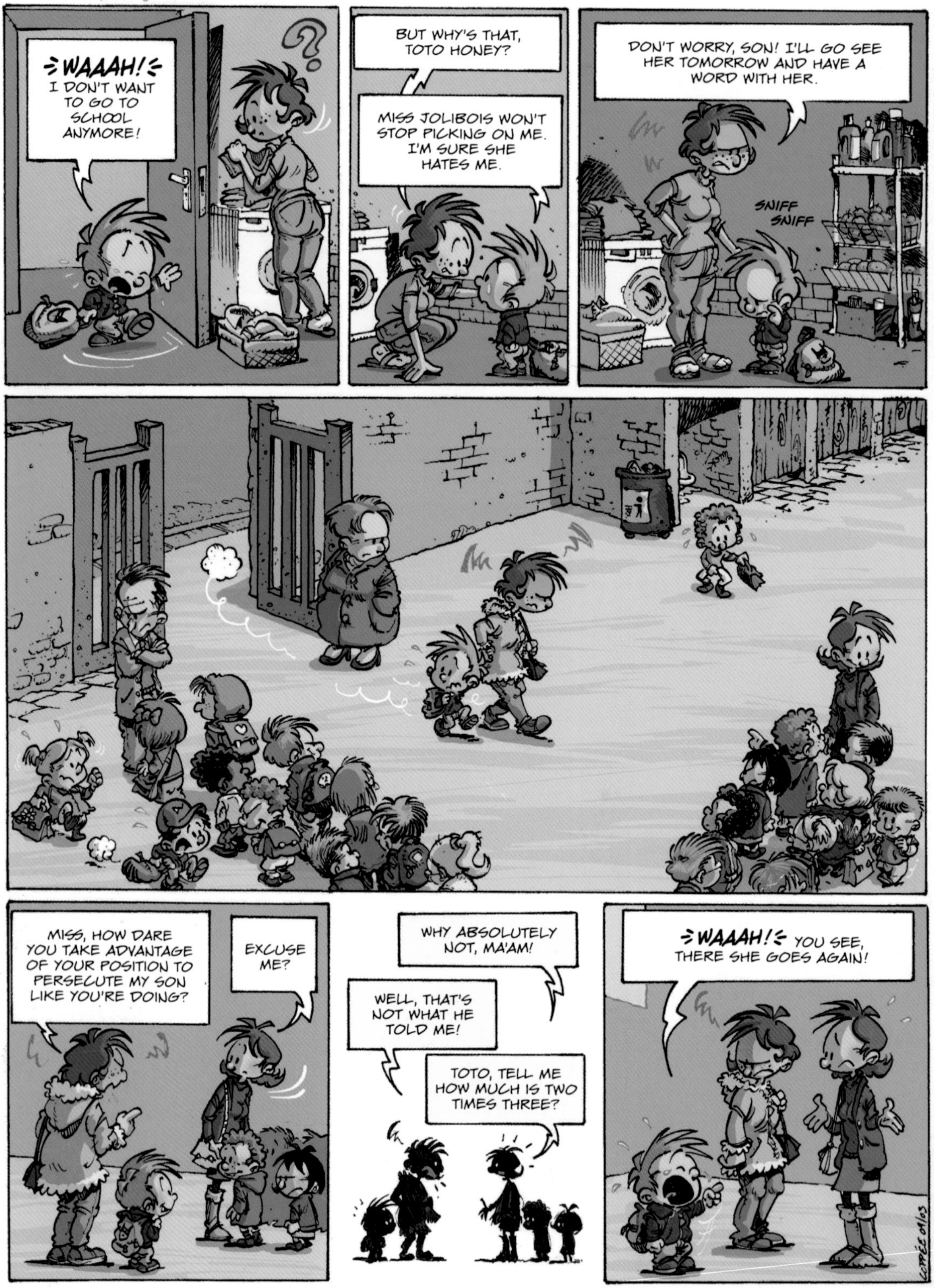

WAAAH! I DON'T WANT TO GO TO SCHOOL ANYMORE!
BUT WHY'S THAT, TOTO HONEY?
MISS JOLIBOIS WON'T STOP PICKING ON ME. I'M SURE SHE HATES ME.
DON'T WORRY, SON! I'LL GO SEE HER TOMORROW AND HAVE A WORD WITH HER.
SNIFF SNIFF
MISS, HOW DARE YOU TAKE ADVANTAGE OF YOUR POSITION TO PERSECUTE MY SON LIKE YOU'RE DOING?
EXCUSE ME?
WHY ABSOLUTELY NOT, MA'AM!
WELL, THAT'S NOT WHAT HE TOLD ME!
TOTO, TELL ME HOW MUCH IS TWO TIMES THREE?
WAAAH! YOU SEE, THERE SHE GOES AGAIN!

"The Changing Room"

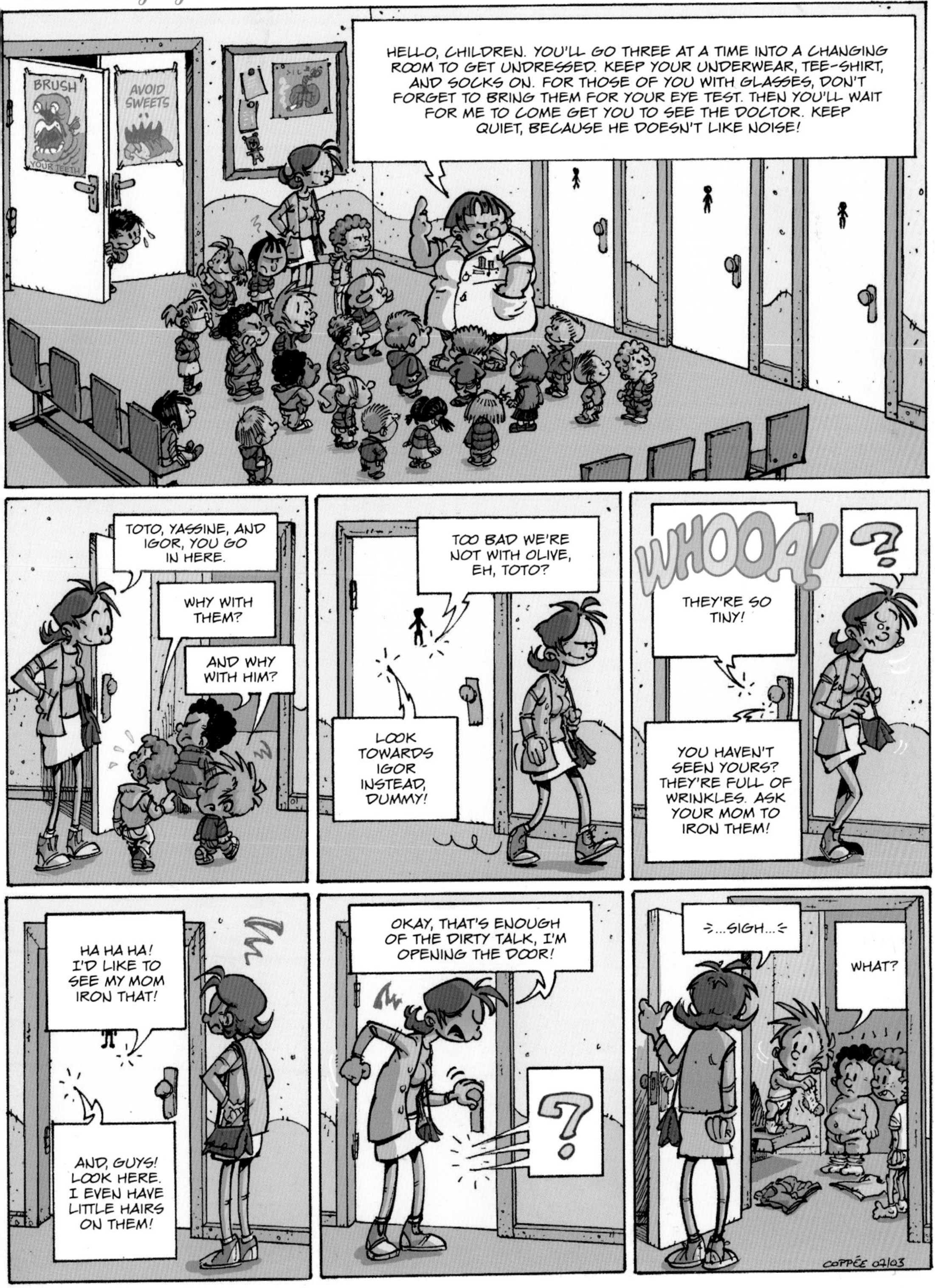

HELLO, CHILDREN. YOU'LL GO THREE AT A TIME INTO A CHANGING ROOM TO GET UNDRESSED. KEEP YOUR UNDERWEAR, TEE-SHIRT, AND SOCKS ON. FOR THOSE OF YOU WITH GLASSES, DON'T FORGET TO BRING THEM FOR YOUR EYE TEST. THEN YOU'LL WAIT FOR ME TO COME GET YOU TO SEE THE DOCTOR. KEEP QUIET, BECAUSE HE DOESN'T LIKE NOISE!
BRUSH YOUR TEETH
AVOID SWEETS
TOTO, YASSINE, AND IGOR, YOU GO IN HERE.
WHY WITH THEM?
AND WHY WITH HIM?
TOO BAD WE'RE NOT WITH OLIVE, EH, TOTO?
LOOK TOWARDS IGOR INSTEAD, DUMMY!
WHOOA!
?
THEY'RE SO TINY!
YOU HAVEN'T SEEN YOURS? THEY'RE FULL OF WRINKLES. ASK YOUR MOM TO IRON THEM!
HA HA HA! I'D LIKE TO SEE MY MOM IRON THAT!
AND, GUYS! LOOK HERE. I EVEN HAVE LITTLE HAIRS ON THEM!
OKAY, THAT'S ENOUGH OF THE DIRTY TALK, I'M OPENING THE DOOR!
?
...SIGH...
WHAT?
COPPÉE 07/03

"A Logical Method"

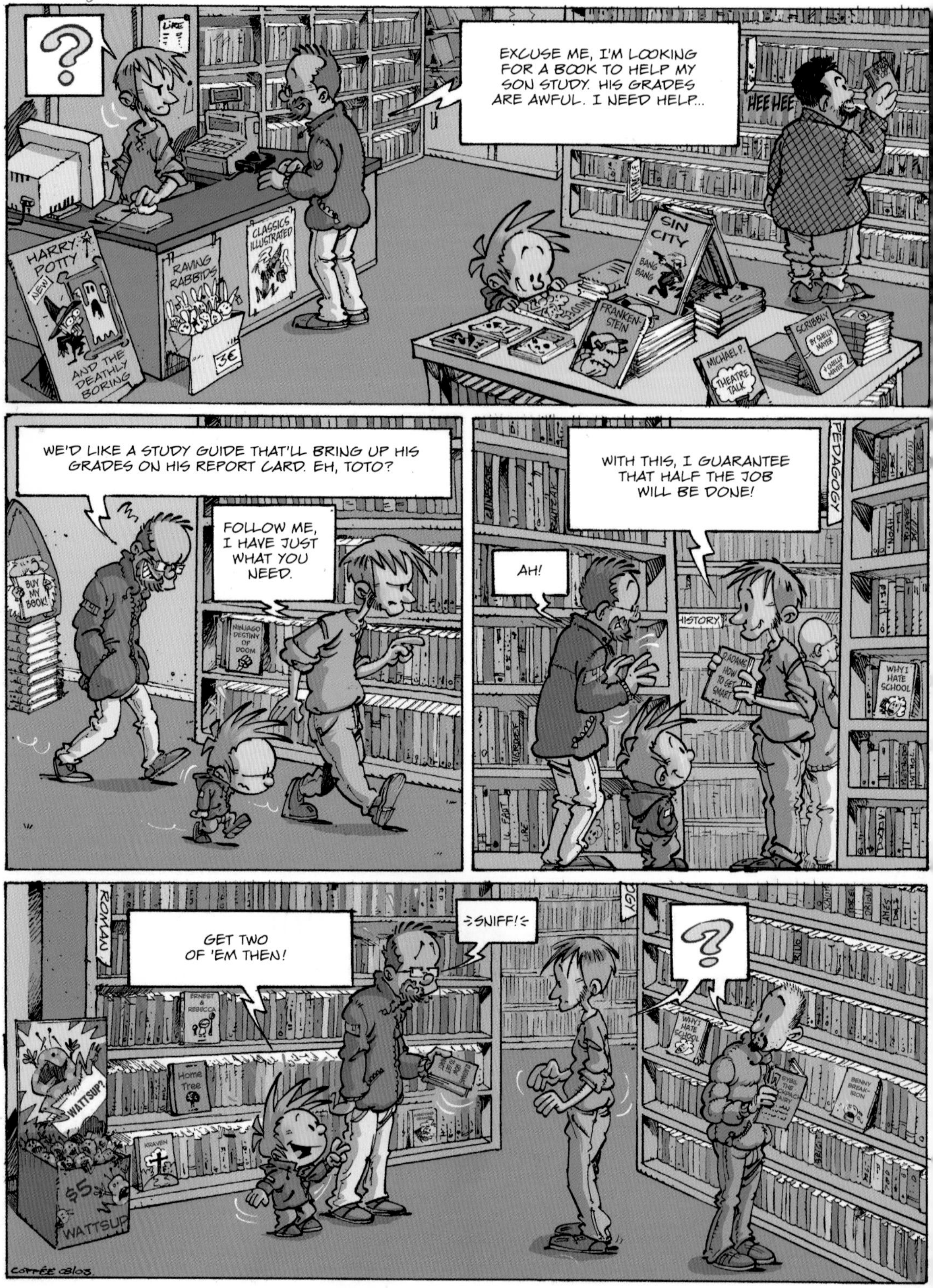
?
EXCUSE ME, I'M LOOKING FOR A BOOK TO HELP MY SON STUDY. HIS GRADES ARE AWFUL. I NEED HELP...
HEE HEE
SIN CITY
FRANKEN-STEIN
HARRY POTTY AND THE DEATHLY BORING
RAVING RABBIDS
CLASSICS ILLUSTRATED
MICHAEL P. THEATRE TALK
SCRIBBLY
WE'D LIKE A STUDY GUIDE THAT'LL BRING UP HIS GRADES ON HIS REPORT CARD. EH, TOTO?
FOLLOW ME, I HAVE JUST WHAT YOU NEED.
BUY MY BOOK!
NINJAGO DESTINY OF DOOM
WITH THIS, I GUARANTEE THAT HALF THE JOB WILL BE DONE!
AH!
PEDAGOGY
HISTORY
HOW TO GET SMART
WHY I HATE SCHOOL
GET TWO OF 'EM THEN!
SNIFF!
?
ROMAN
ERNEST & REBECCA
Home Tree
WATTSUP?
$5
WATTSUP
WHY I HATE SCHOOL
BENNY BREAK-IRON

"Seeing Red"

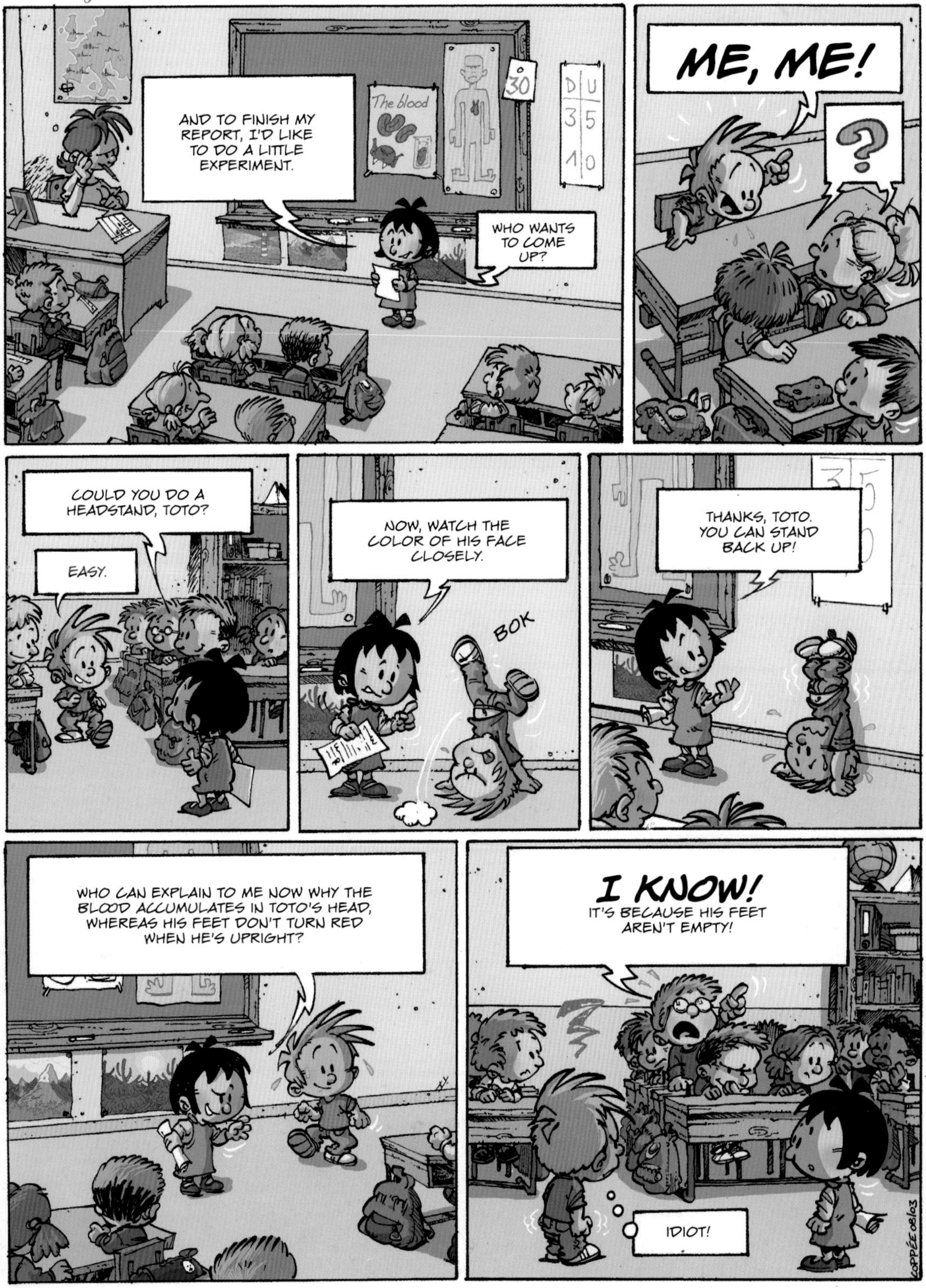

The blood
30
D U
3 5
1 0
AND TO FINISH MY REPORT, I'D LIKE TO DO A LITTLE EXPERIMENT.
WHO WANTS TO COME UP?
ME, ME!
?
COULD YOU DO A HEADSTAND, TOTO?
EASY.
NOW, WATCH THE COLOR OF HIS FACE CLOSELY.
BOK
THANKS, TOTO. YOU CAN STAND BACK UP!
WHO CAN EXPLAIN TO ME NOW WHY THE BLOOD ACCUMULATES IN TOTO'S HEAD, WHEREAS HIS FEET DON'T TURN RED WHEN HE'S UPRIGHT?
I KNOW!
IT'S BECAUSE HIS FEET AREN'T EMPTY!
IDIOT!
COPPÉE 08/03

"Find the Mistake"

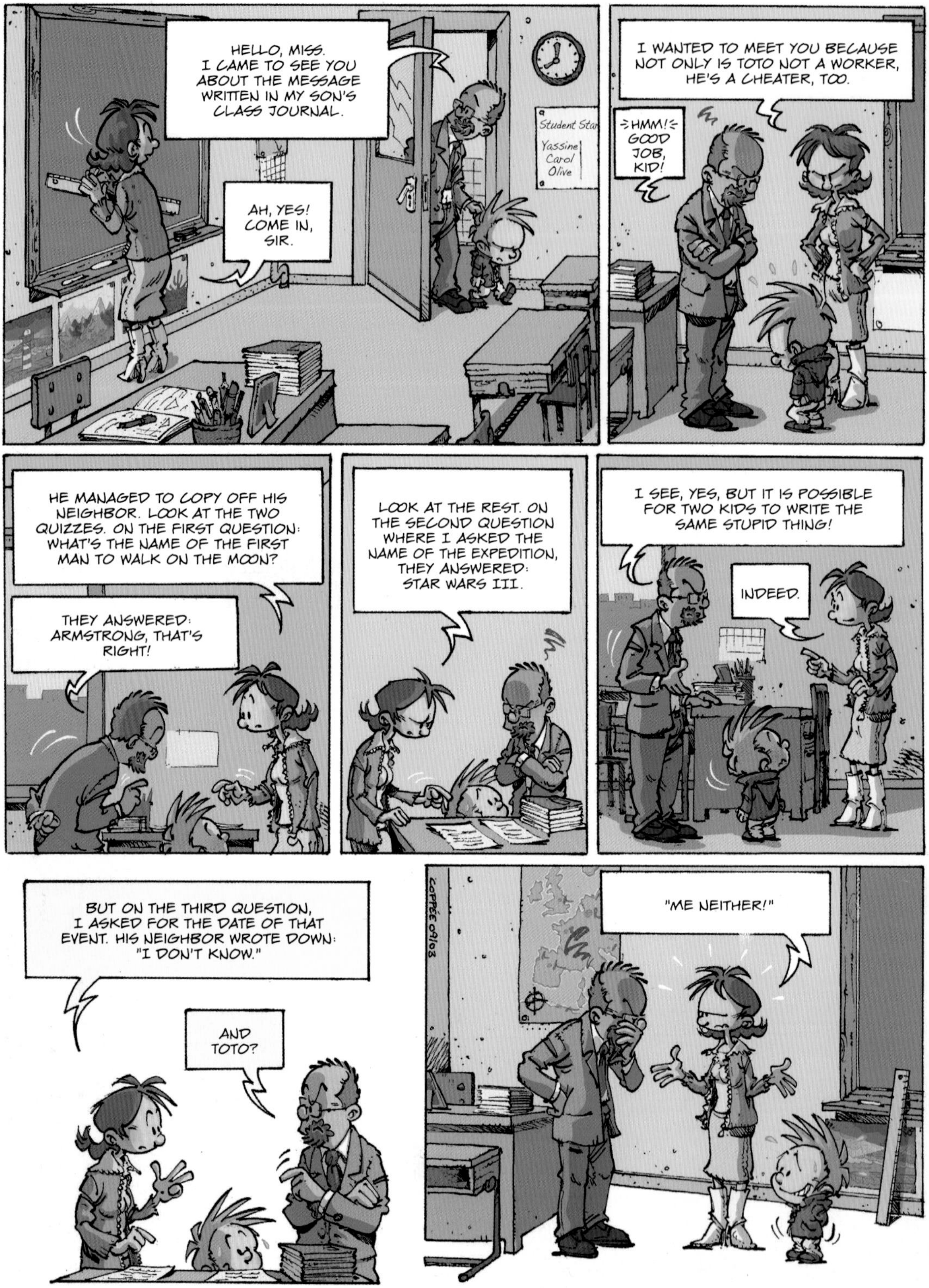
HELLO, MISS. I CAME TO SEE YOU ABOUT THE MESSAGE WRITTEN IN MY SON'S CLASS JOURNAL.
AH, YES! COME IN, SIR.
Student Star
Yassine
Carol
Olive
I WANTED TO MEET YOU BECAUSE NOT ONLY IS TOTO NOT A WORKER, HE'S A CHEATER, TOO.
HMM! GOOD JOB, KID!
HE MANAGED TO COPY OFF HIS NEIGHBOR. LOOK AT THE TWO QUIZZES. ON THE FIRST QUESTION: WHAT'S THE NAME OF THE FIRST MAN TO WALK ON THE MOON?
THEY ANSWERED: ARMSTRONG, THAT'S RIGHT!
LOOK AT THE REST. ON THE SECOND QUESTION WHERE I ASKED THE NAME OF THE EXPEDITION, THEY ANSWERED: STAR WARS III.
I SEE, YES, BUT IT IS POSSIBLE FOR TWO KIDS TO WRITE THE SAME STUPID THING!
INDEED.
BUT ON THE THIRD QUESTION, I ASKED FOR THE DATE OF THAT EVENT. HIS NEIGHBOR WROTE DOWN: "I DON'T KNOW."
AND TOTO?
"ME NEITHER!"
COPPÉE 09/03

"The Hypochondriac"

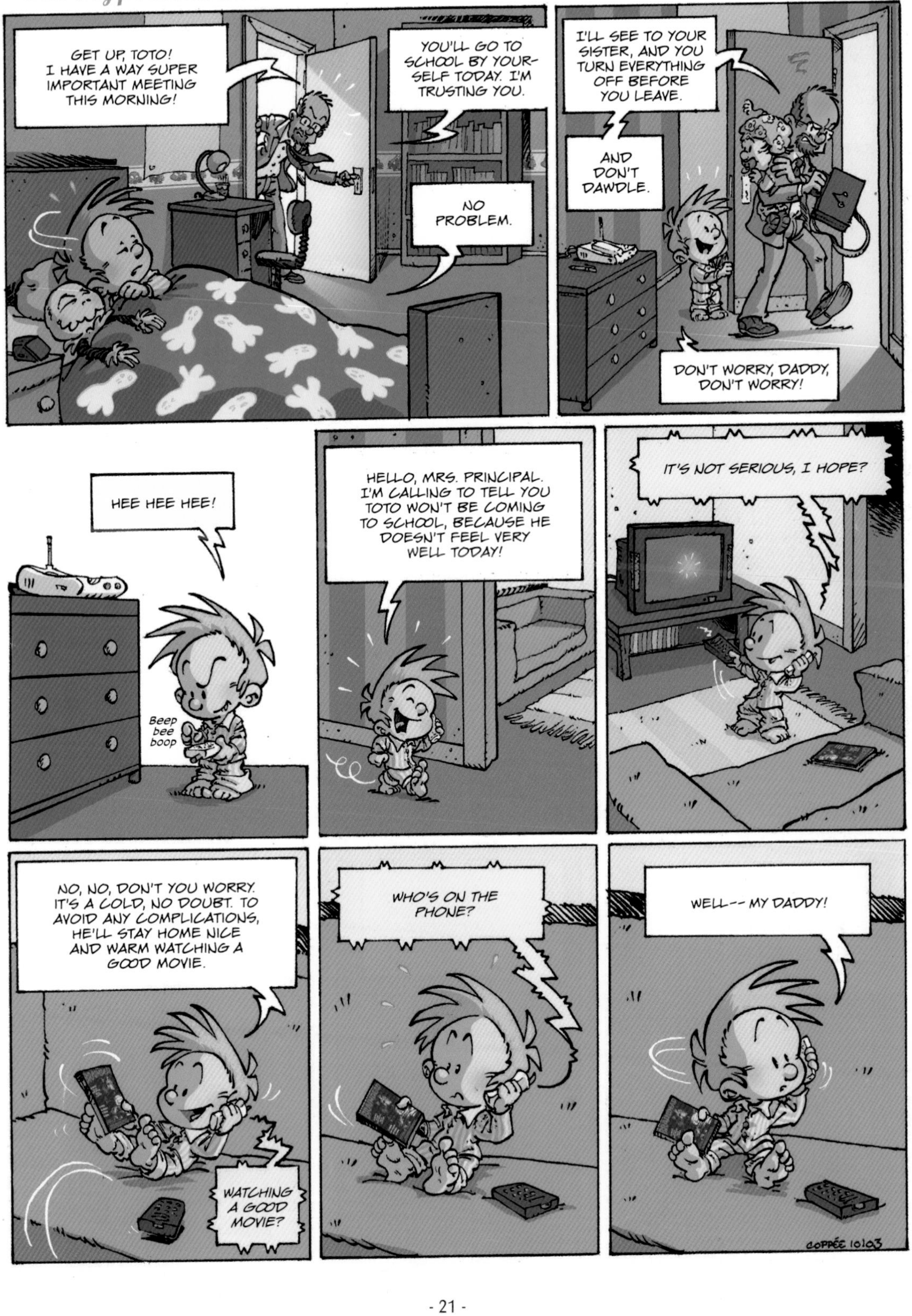
GET UP, TOTO! I HAVE A WAY SUPER IMPORTANT MEETING THIS MORNING!
YOU'LL GO TO SCHOOL BY YOURSELF TODAY. I'M TRUSTING YOU.
NO PROBLEM.
I'LL SEE TO YOUR SISTER, AND YOU TURN EVERYTHING OFF BEFORE YOU LEAVE.
AND DON'T DAWDLE.
DON'T WORRY, DADDY, DON'T WORRY!
HEE HEE HEE!
Beep bee boop
HELLO, MRS. PRINCIPAL. I'M CALLING TO TELL YOU TOTO WON'T BE COMING TO SCHOOL, BECAUSE HE DOESN'T FEEL VERY WELL TODAY!
IT'S NOT SERIOUS, I HOPE?
NO, NO, DON'T YOU WORRY. IT'S A COLD, NO DOUBT. TO AVOID ANY COMPLICATIONS, HE'LL STAY HOME NICE AND WARM WATCHING A GOOD MOVIE.
WATCHING A GOOD MOVIE?
WHO'S ON THE PHONE?
WELL-- MY DADDY!
COPPÉE 10|03

"Report Cards"

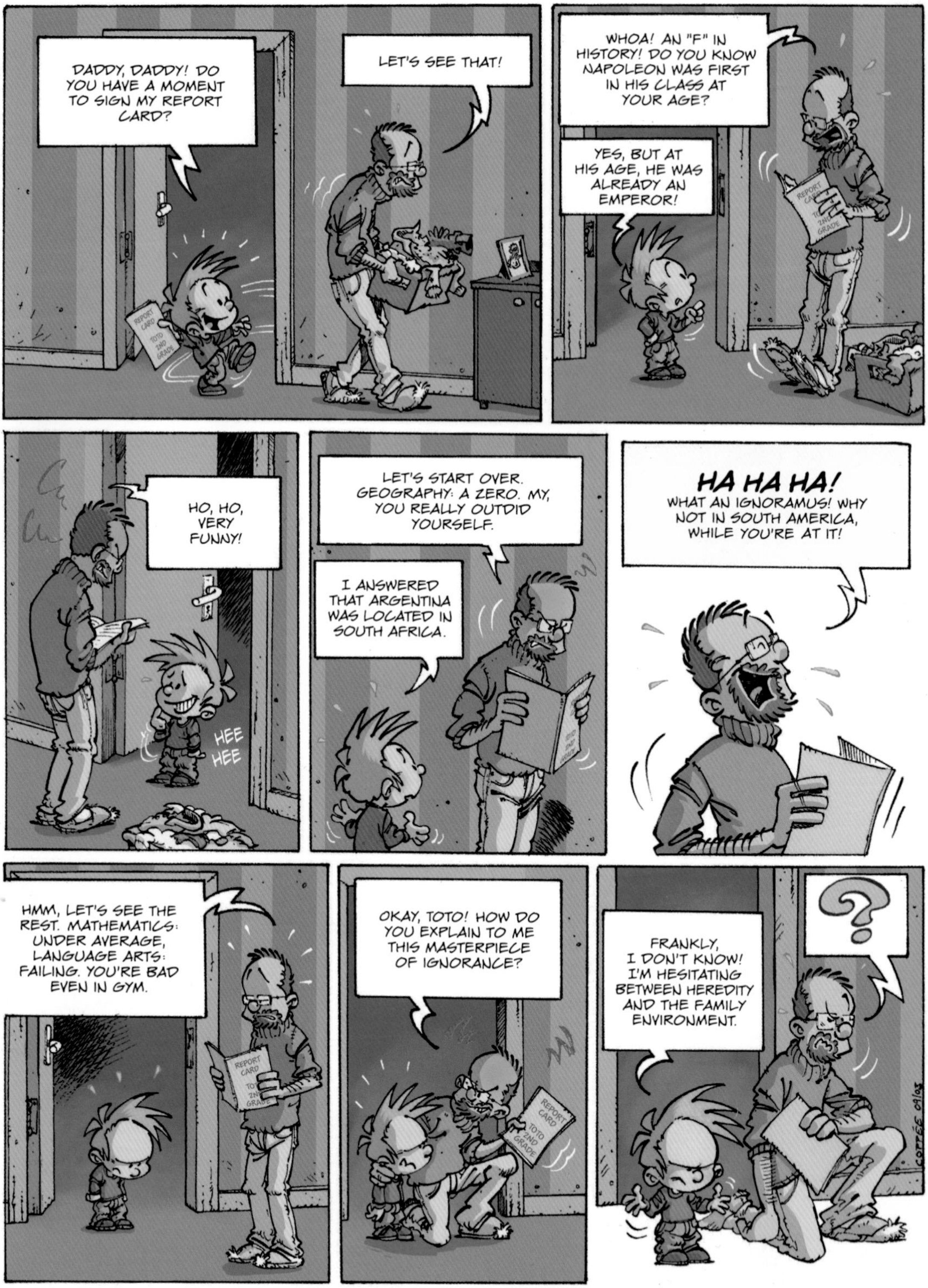
DADDY, DADDY! DO YOU HAVE A MOMENT TO SIGN MY REPORT CARD?
REPORT CARD TOTO 2ND GRADE
LET'S SEE THAT!
WHOA! AN "F" IN HISTORY! DO YOU KNOW NAPOLEON WAS FIRST IN HIS CLASS AT YOUR AGE?
YES, BUT AT HIS AGE, HE WAS ALREADY AN EMPEROR!
REPORT CARD TOTO 2ND GRADE
HO, HO, VERY FUNNY!
HEE HEE
LET'S START OVER. GEOGRAPHY: A ZERO. MY, YOU REALLY OUTDID YOURSELF.
I ANSWERED THAT ARGENTINA WAS LOCATED IN SOUTH AFRICA.
HA HA HA!
WHAT AN IGNORAMUS! WHY NOT IN SOUTH AMERICA, WHILE YOU'RE AT IT!
HMM, LET'S SEE THE REST. MATHEMATICS: UNDER AVERAGE, LANGUAGE ARTS: FAILING. YOU'RE BAD EVEN IN GYM.
REPORT CARD TOTO 2ND GRADE
OKAY, TOTO! HOW DO YOU EXPLAIN TO ME THIS MASTERPIECE OF IGNORANCE?
REPORT CARD TOTO 2ND GRADE
?
FRANKLY, I DON'T KNOW! I'M HESITATING BETWEEN HEREDITY AND THE FAMILY ENVIRONMENT.

"Photo Souvenir"

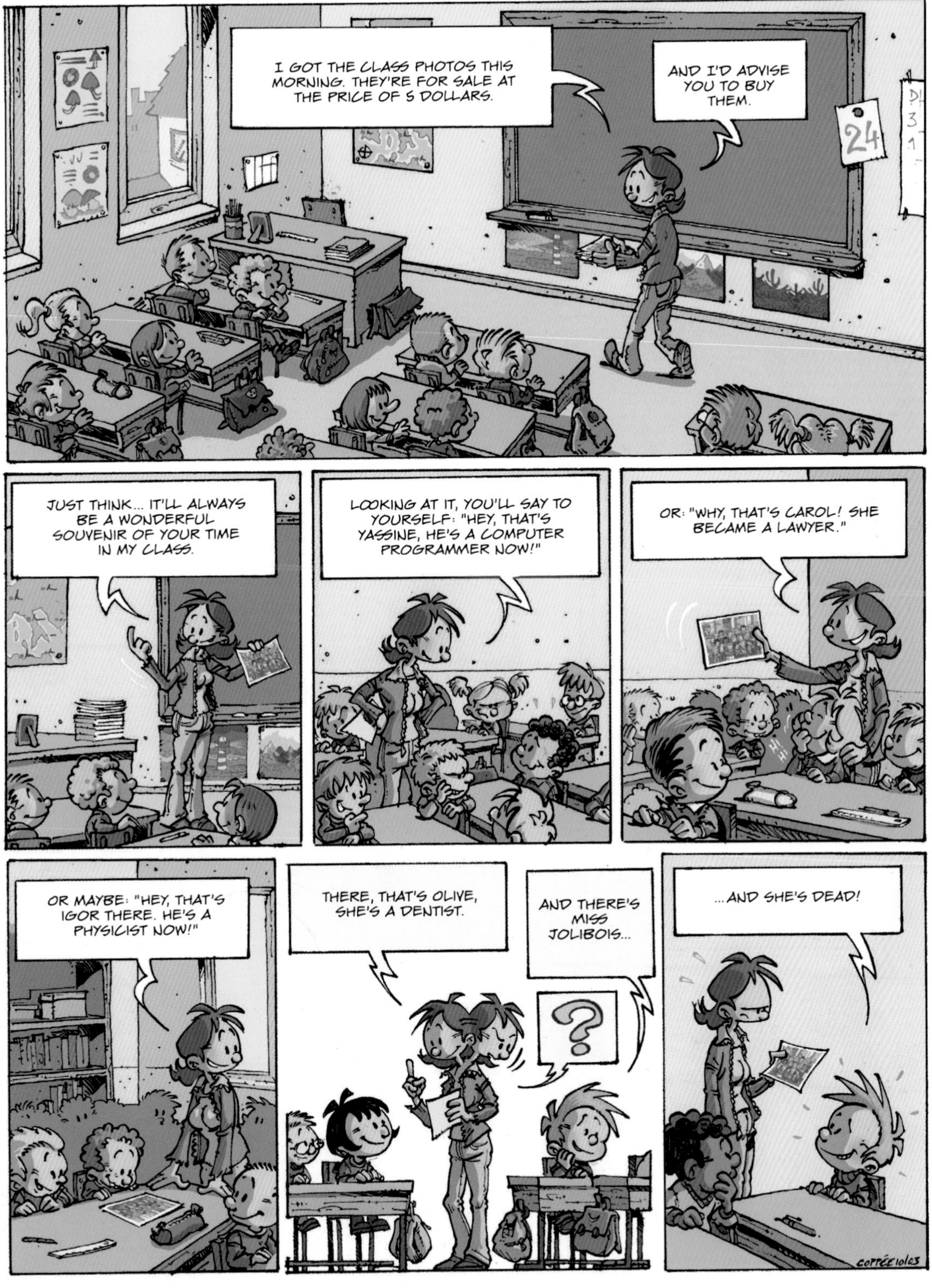

I GOT THE CLASS PHOTOS THIS MORNING. THEY'RE FOR SALE AT THE PRICE OF 5 DOLLARS.
AND I'D ADVISE YOU TO BUY THEM.
24
JUST THINK... IT'LL ALWAYS BE A WONDERFUL SOUVENIR OF YOUR TIME IN MY CLASS.
LOOKING AT IT, YOU'LL SAY TO YOURSELF: "HEY, THAT'S YASSINE, HE'S A COMPUTER PROGRAMMER NOW!"
OR: "WHY, THAT'S CAROL! SHE BECAME A LAWYER."
OR MAYBE: "HEY, THAT'S IGOR THERE. HE'S A PHYSICIST NOW!"
THERE, THAT'S OLIVE, SHE'S A DENTIST.
AND THERE'S MISS JOLIBOIS...
?
...AND SHE'S DEAD!
COPPÉE 10/03

"Better Safe than Sorry"

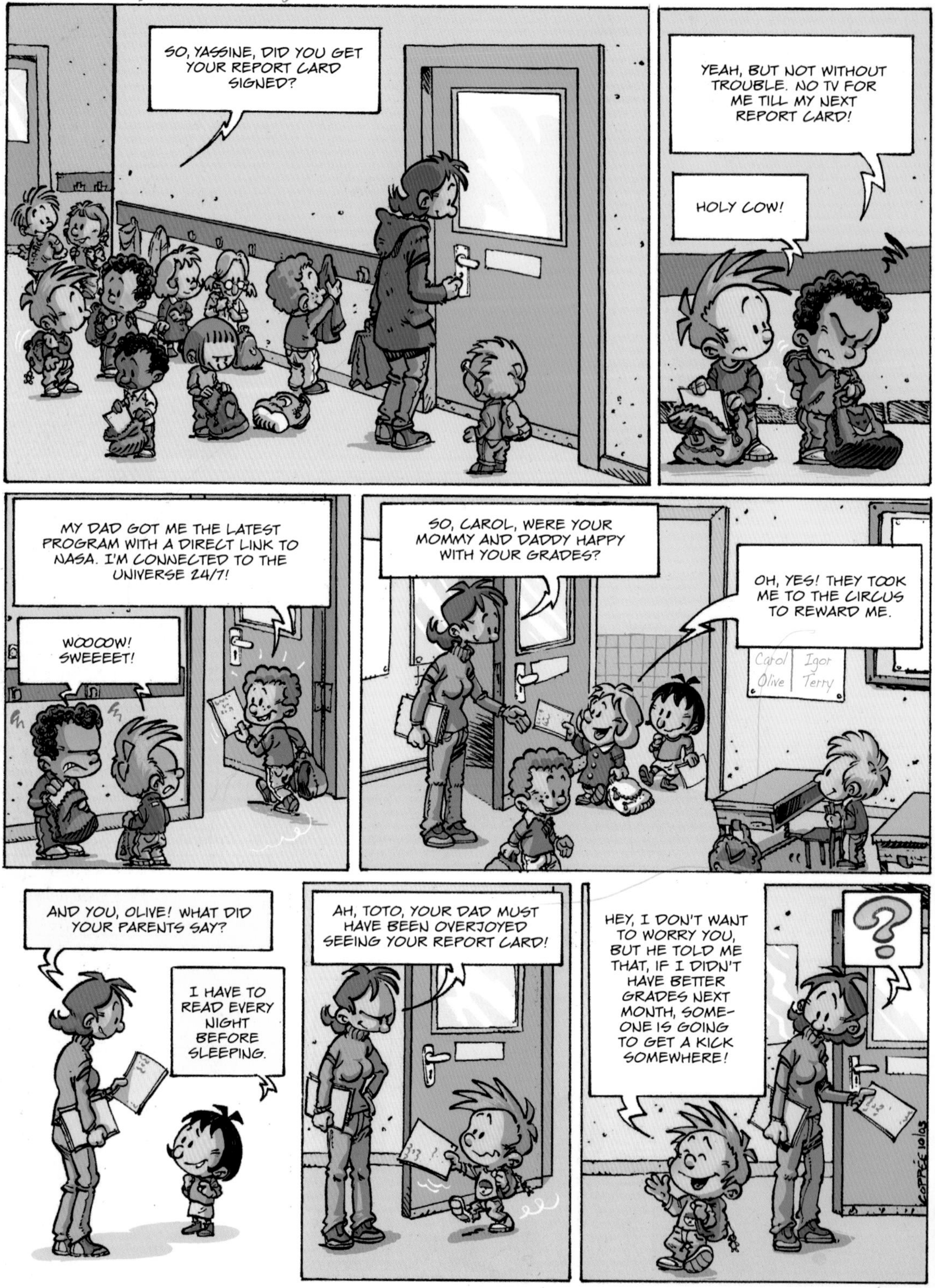

SO, YASSINE, DID YOU GET YOUR REPORT CARD SIGNED?
YEAH, BUT NOT WITHOUT TROUBLE. NO TV FOR ME TILL MY NEXT REPORT CARD!
HOLY COW!
MY DAD GOT ME THE LATEST PROGRAM WITH A DIRECT LINK TO NASA. I'M CONNECTED TO THE UNIVERSE 24/7!
WOOOOW! SWEEEET!
SO, CAROL, WERE YOUR MOMMY AND DADDY HAPPY WITH YOUR GRADES?
OH, YES! THEY TOOK ME TO THE CIRCUS TO REWARD ME.
Carol Igor
Olive Terry
AND YOU, OLIVE! WHAT DID YOUR PARENTS SAY?
I HAVE TO READ EVERY NIGHT BEFORE SLEEPING.
AH, TOTO, YOUR DAD MUST HAVE BEEN OVERJOYED SEEING YOUR REPORT CARD!
HEY, I DON'T WANT TO WORRY YOU, BUT HE TOLD ME THAT, IF I DIDN'T HAVE BETTER GRADES NEXT MONTH, SOME-ONE IS GOING TO GET A KICK SOMEWHERE!
?

"Shut Up"

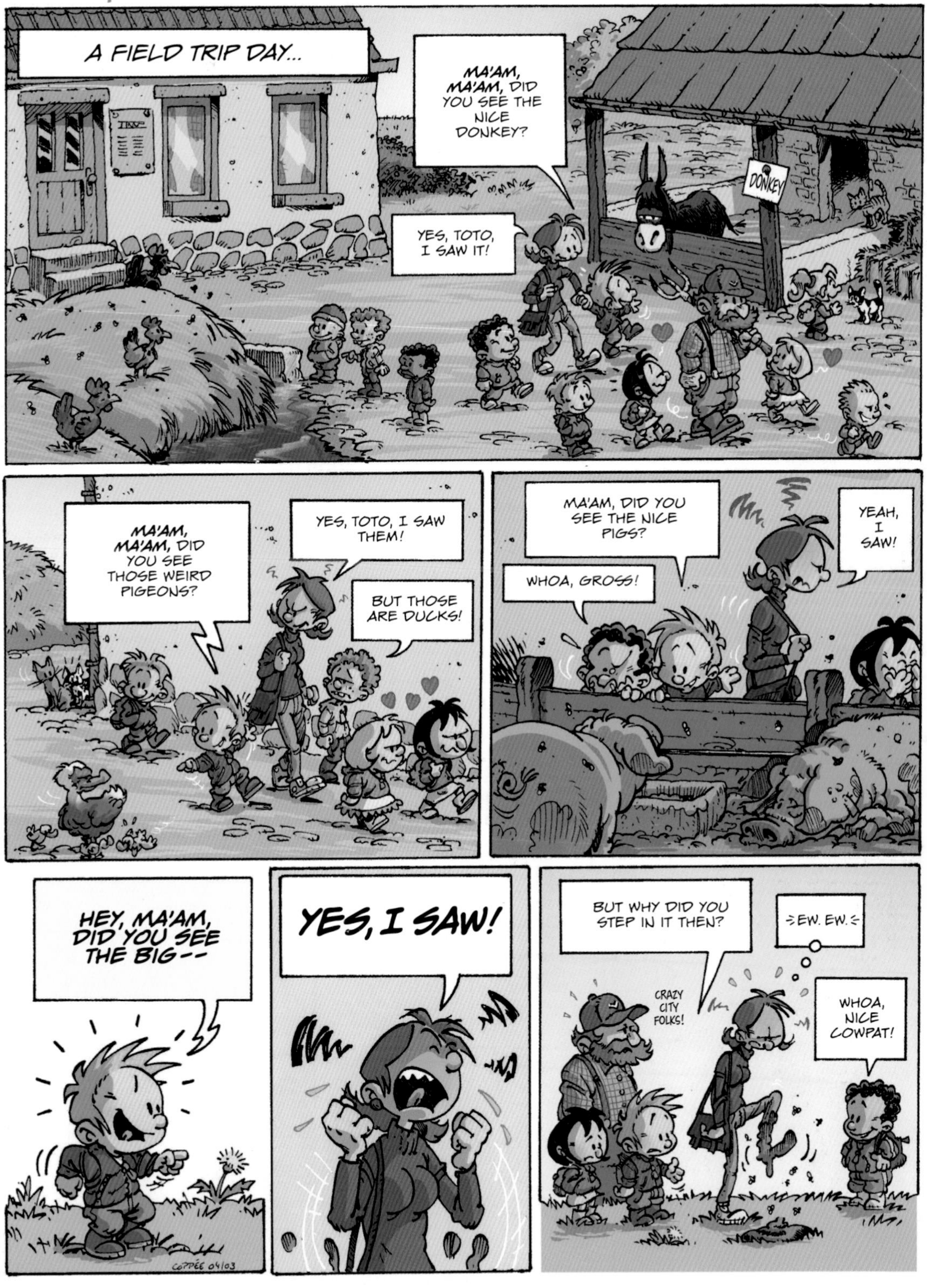
A FIELD TRIP DAY...
MA'AM, MA'AM, DID YOU SEE THE NICE DONKEY?
DONKEY
YES, TOTO, I SAW IT!
MA'AM, MA'AM, DID YOU SEE THOSE WEIRD PIGEONS?
YES, TOTO, I SAW THEM!
BUT THOSE ARE DUCKS!
MA'AM, DID YOU SEE THE NICE PIGS?
WHOA, GROSS!
YEAH, I SAW!
HEY, MA'AM, DID YOU SEE THE BIG--
YES, I SAW!
BUT WHY DID YOU STEP IN IT THEN?
EW. EW.
CRAZY CITY FOLKS!
WHOA, NICE COWPAT!
COPPÉE 04/03

"Draw Me Two Cows"

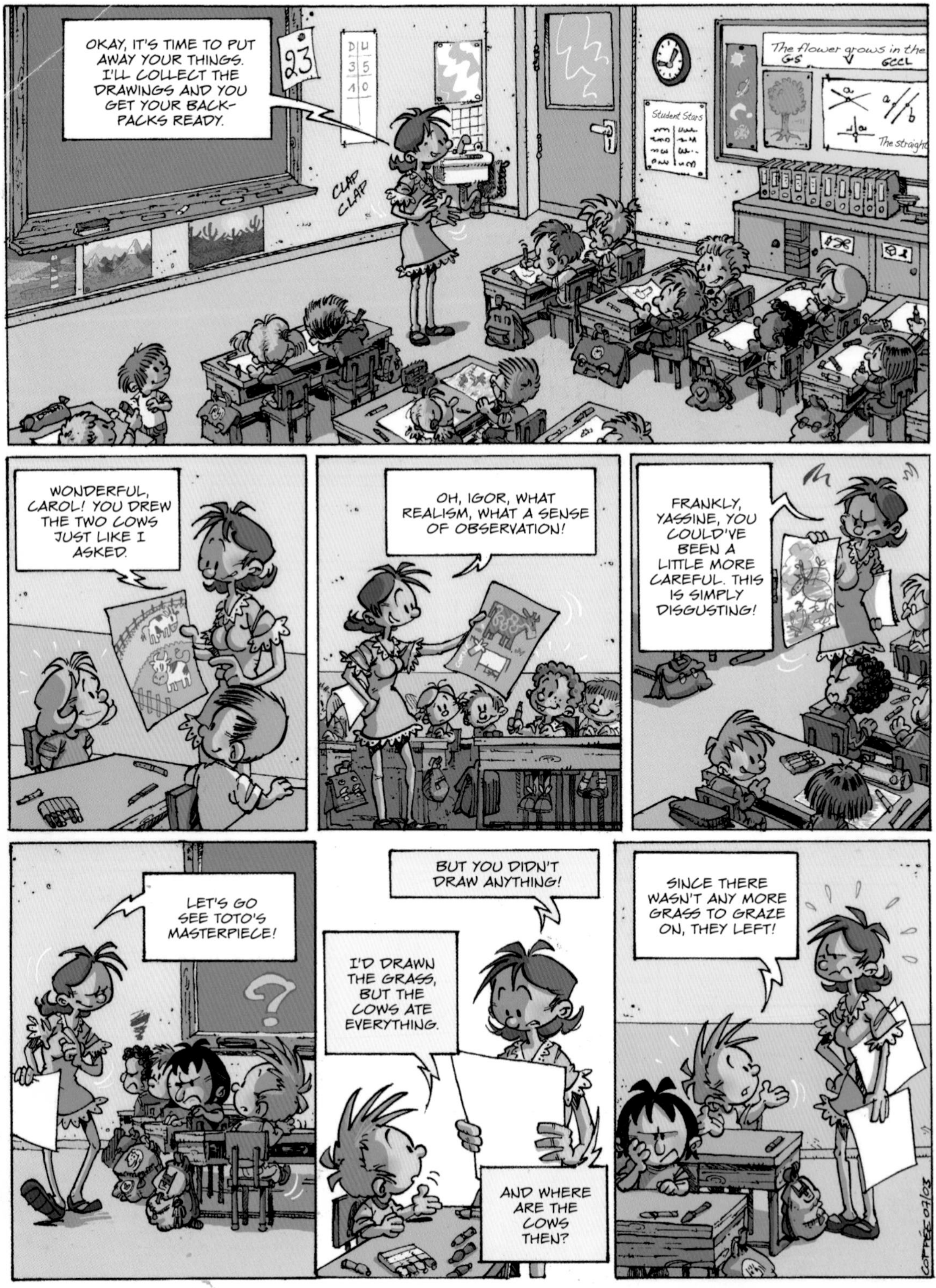
OKAY, IT'S TIME TO PUT AWAY YOUR THINGS. I'LL COLLECT THE DRAWINGS AND YOU GET YOUR BACK-PACKS READY.
23
CLAP CLAP
Student Stars
The flower grows in the
WONDERFUL, CAROL! YOU DREW THE TWO COWS JUST LIKE I ASKED.
OH, IGOR, WHAT REALISM, WHAT A SENSE OF OBSERVATION!
FRANKLY, YASSINE, YOU COULD'VE BEEN A LITTLE MORE CAREFUL. THIS IS SIMPLY DISGUSTING!
LET'S GO SEE TOTO'S MASTERPIECE!
BUT YOU DIDN'T DRAW ANYTHING!
I'D DRAWN THE GRASS, BUT THE COWS ATE EVERYTHING.
AND WHERE ARE THE COWS THEN?
SINCE THERE WASN'T ANY MORE GRASS TO GRAZE ON, THEY LEFT!
COPPÉE 07/03

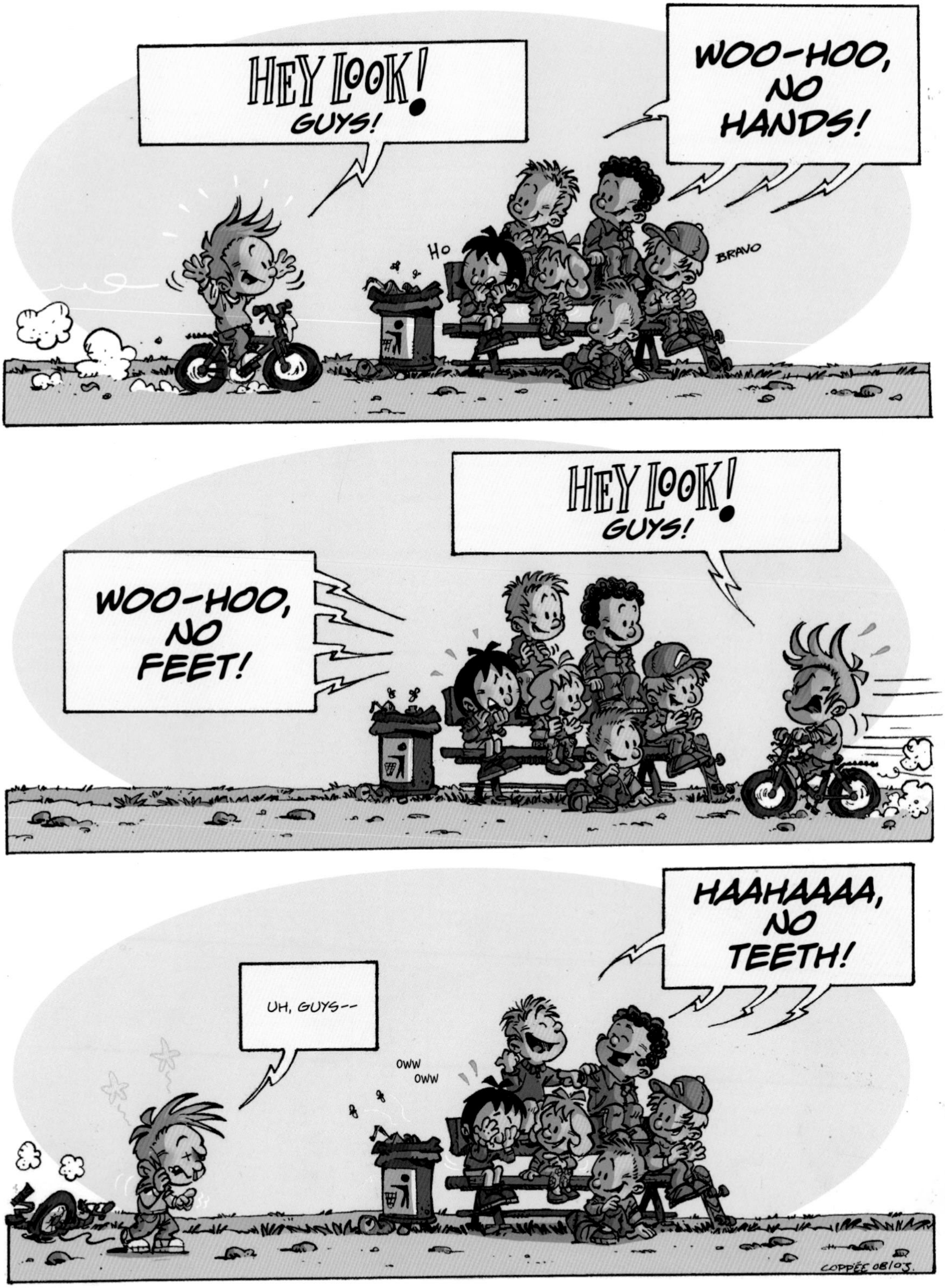
HEY LOOK! GUYS!
HO
BRAVO
WOO-HOO, NO HANDS!
HEY LOOK! GUYS!
WOO-HOO, NO FEET!
UH, GUYS--
OWW OWW
HAAHAAAA, NO TEETH!
COPPÉE 08/03.

"Red Currants"

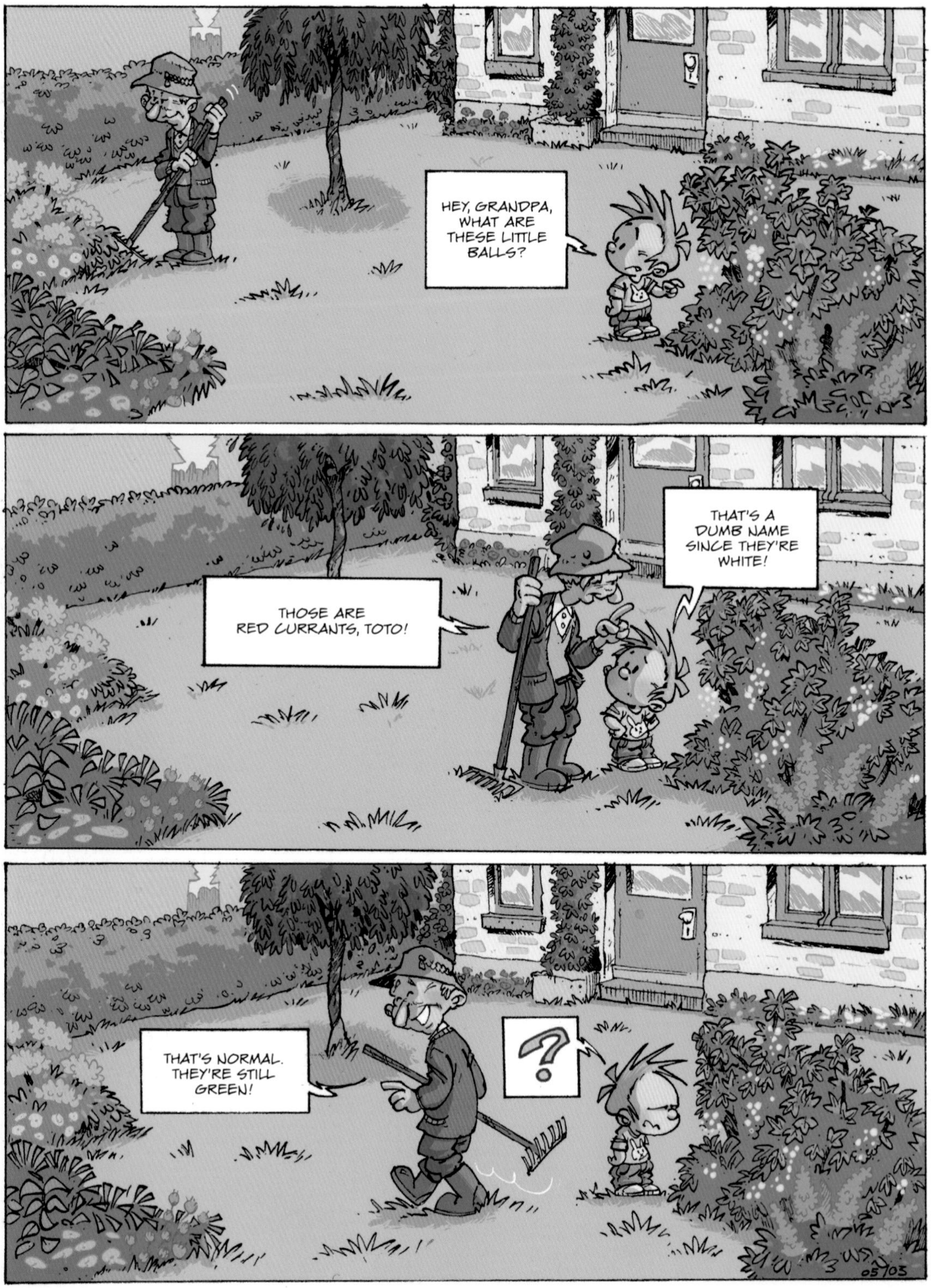
HEY, GRANDPA, WHAT ARE THESE LITTLE BALLS?
THOSE ARE RED CURRANTS, TOTO!
THAT'S A DUMB NAME SINCE THEY'RE WHITE!
THAT'S NORMAL. THEY'RE STILL GREEN!
?
05/03

"End-of-the-Year Gift"

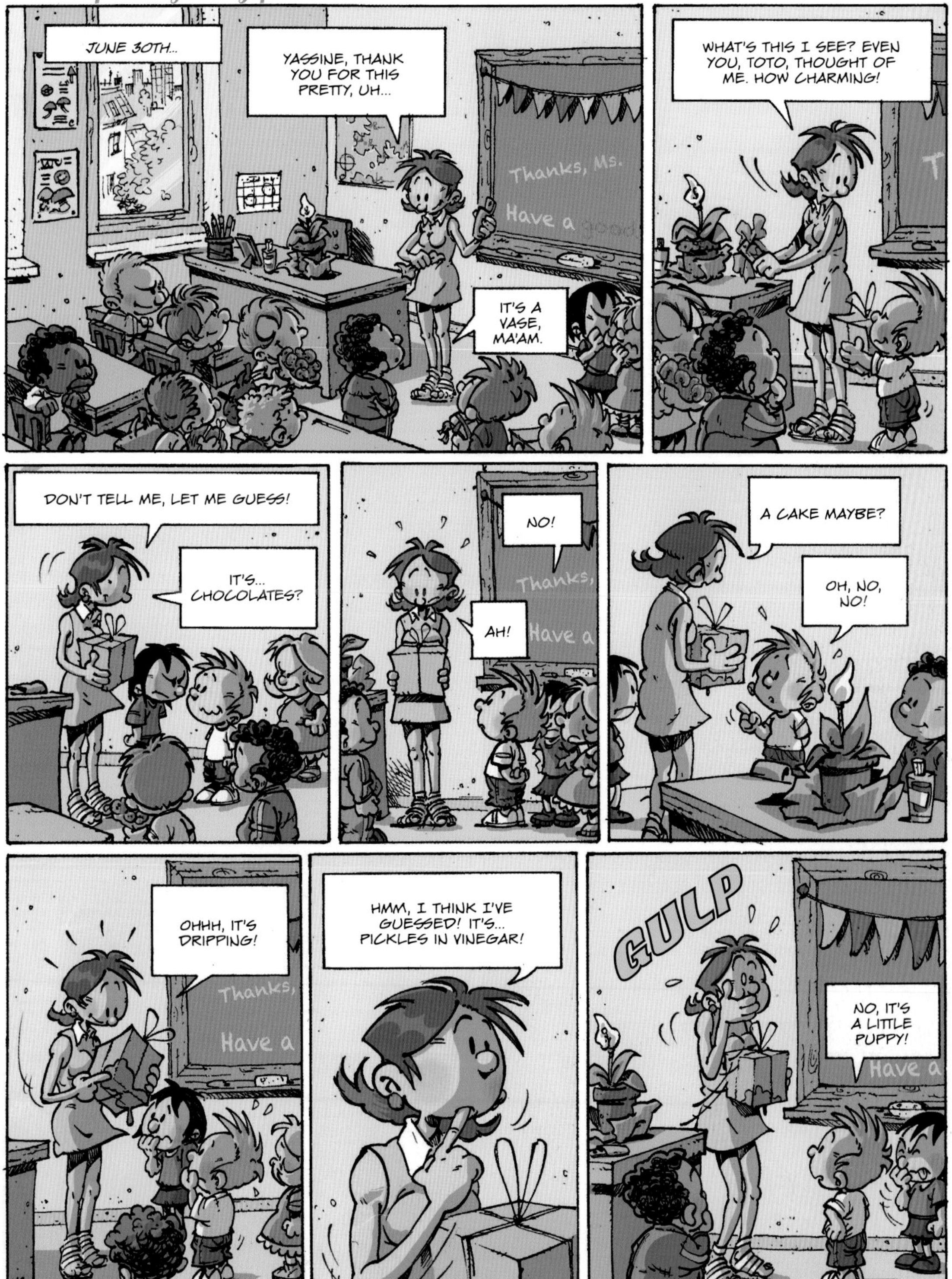
JUNE 30TH...
YASSINE, THANK YOU FOR THIS PRETTY, UH...
Thanks, Ms.
Have a good
IT'S A VASE, MA'AM.
WHAT'S THIS I SEE? EVEN YOU, TOTO, THOUGHT OF ME. HOW CHARMING!
DON'T TELL ME, LET ME GUESS!
IT'S... CHOCOLATES?
NO!
Thanks,
Have a
AH!
A CAKE MAYBE?
OH, NO, NO!
OHHH, IT'S DRIPPING!
Thanks,
Have a
HMM, I THINK I'VE GUESSED! IT'S... PICKLES IN VINEGAR!
GULP
NO, IT'S A LITTLE PUPPY!
Have a
COPPÉE 04/03

"Questions for a Champion-- The Finale"

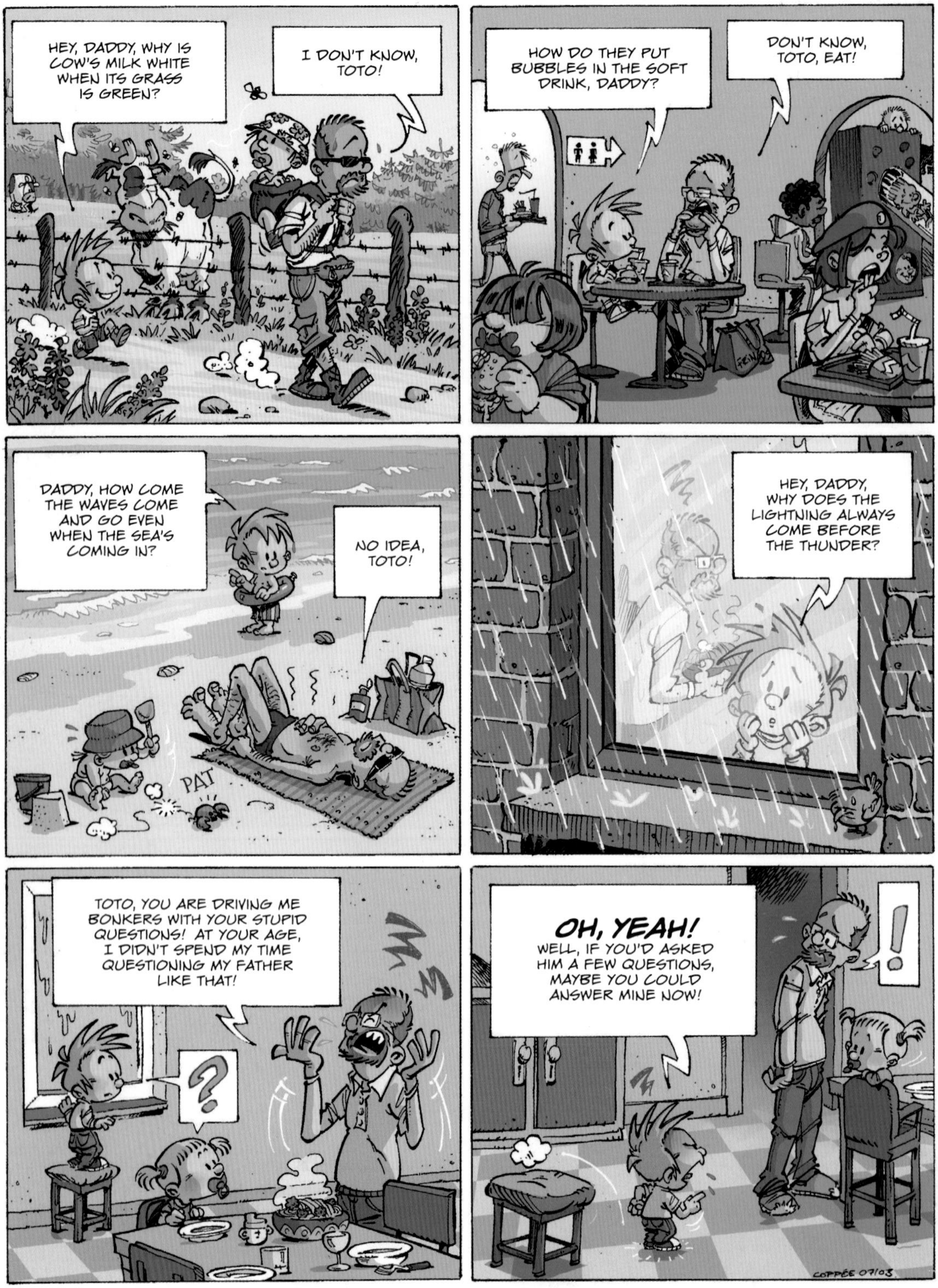
HEY, DADDY, WHY IS COW'S MILK WHITE WHEN ITS GRASS IS GREEN?
I DON'T KNOW, TOTO!
HOW DO THEY PUT BUBBLES IN THE SOFT DRINK, DADDY?
DON'T KNOW, TOTO, EAT!
DADDY, HOW COME THE WAVES COME AND GO EVEN WHEN THE SEA'S COMING IN?
NO IDEA, TOTO!
PAT
HEY, DADDY, WHY DOES THE LIGHTNING ALWAYS COME BEFORE THE THUNDER?
TOTO, YOU ARE DRIVING ME BONKERS WITH YOUR STUPID QUESTIONS! AT YOUR AGE, I DIDN'T SPEND MY TIME QUESTIONING MY FATHER LIKE THAT!
?
OH, YEAH!
WELL, IF YOU'D ASKED HIM A FEW QUESTIONS, MAYBE YOU COULD ANSWER MINE NOW!
!

"Quick Directions"

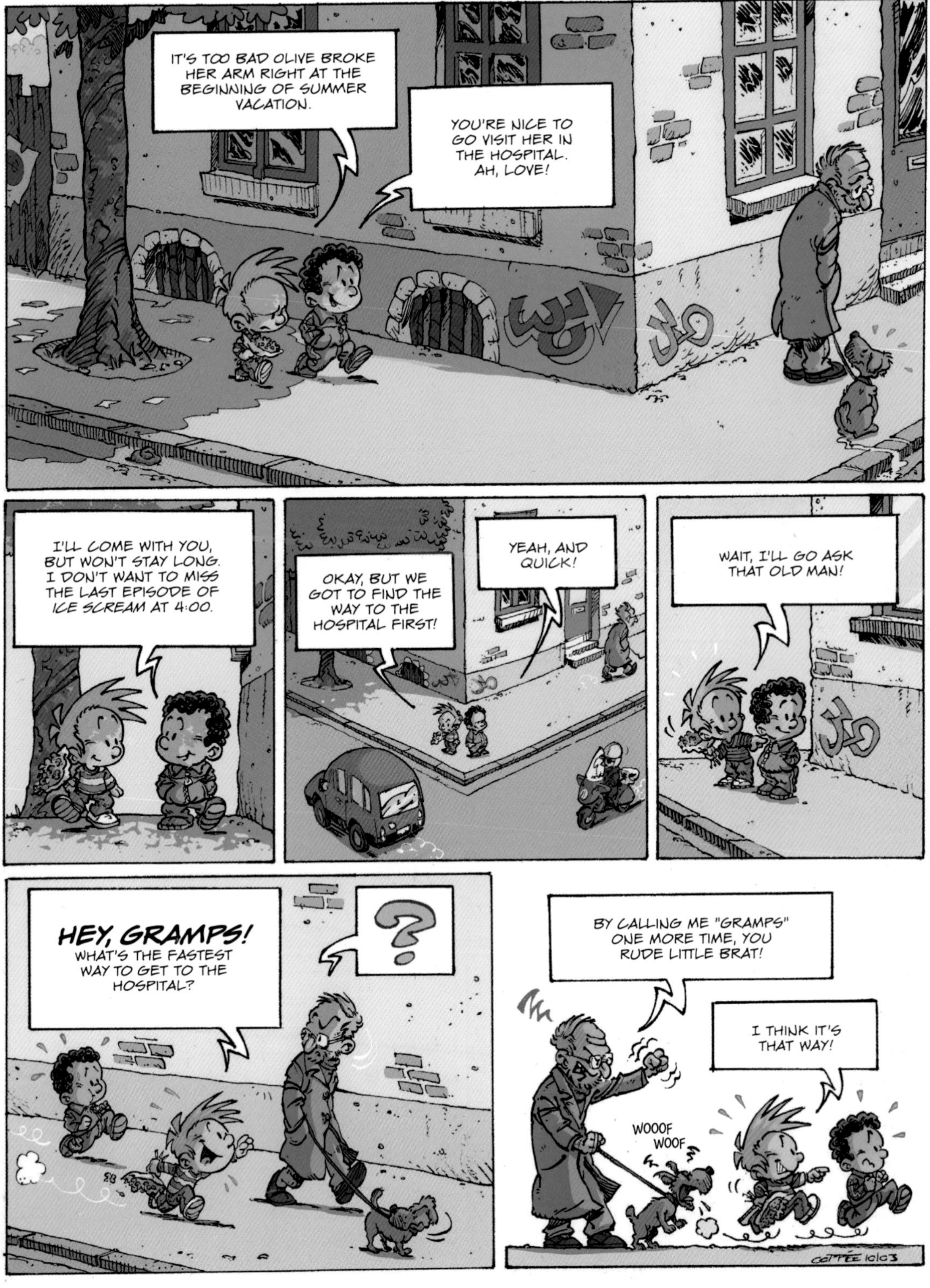

IT'S TOO BAD OLIVE BROKE HER ARM RIGHT AT THE BEGINNING OF SUMMER VACATION.
YOU'RE NICE TO GO VISIT HER IN THE HOSPITAL. AH, LOVE!
I'LL COME WITH YOU, BUT WON'T STAY LONG. I DON'T WANT TO MISS THE LAST EPISODE OF ICE SCREAM AT 4:00.
OKAY, BUT WE GOT TO FIND THE WAY TO THE HOSPITAL FIRST!
YEAH, AND QUICK!
WAIT, I'LL GO ASK THAT OLD MAN!
HEY, GRAMPS! WHAT'S THE FASTEST WAY TO GET TO THE HOSPITAL?
?
BY CALLING ME "GRAMPS" ONE MORE TIME, YOU RUDE LITTLE BRAT!
I THINK IT'S THAT WAY!
WOOOF WOOF
COTTEE 10/03

"There Once was a Little Ship"

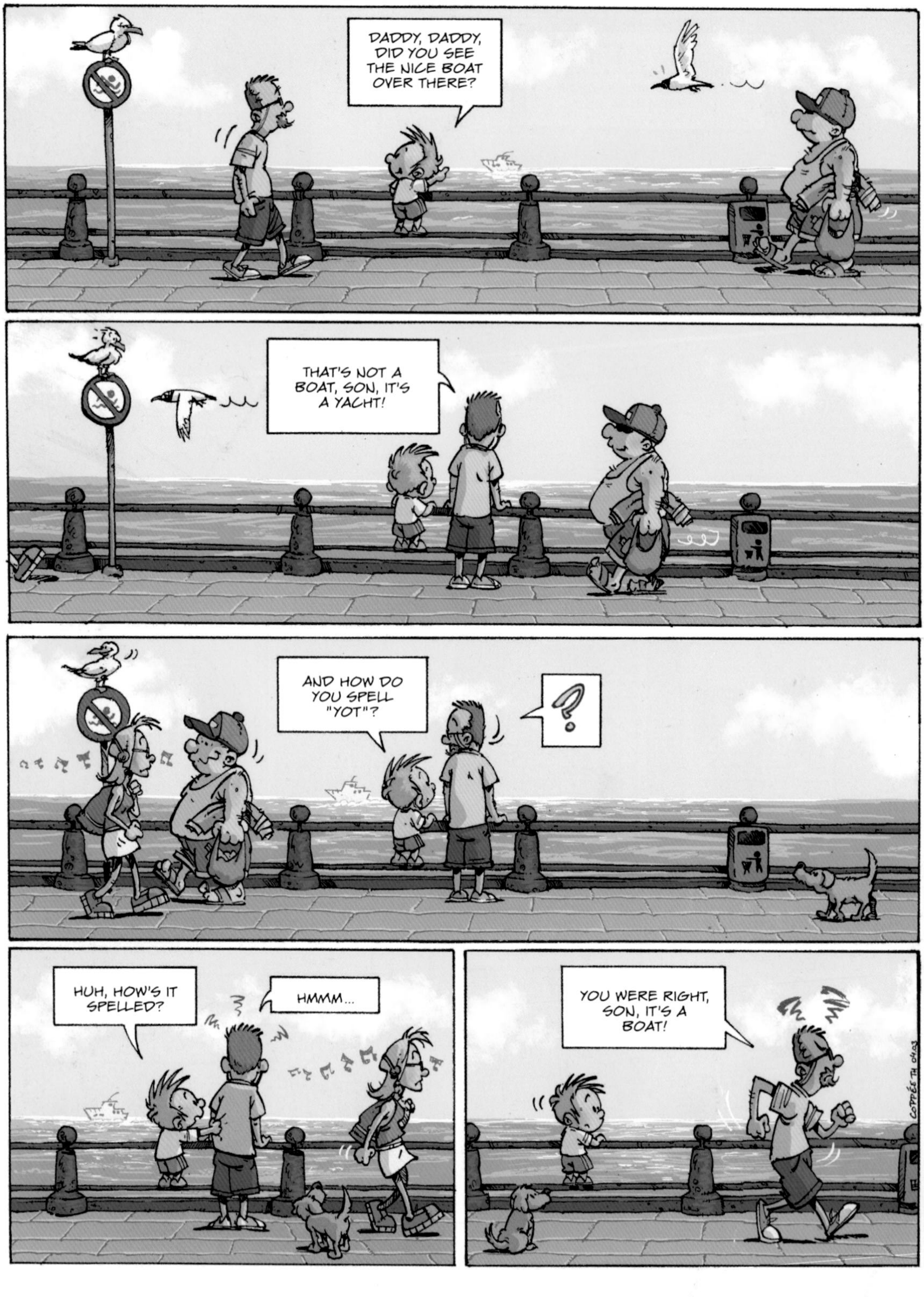

DADDY, DADDY, DID YOU SEE THE NICE BOAT OVER THERE?
THAT'S NOT A BOAT, SON, IT'S A YACHT!
AND HOW DO YOU SPELL "YOT"?
?
HUH, HOW'S IT SPELLED?
HMMM...
YOU WERE RIGHT, SON, IT'S A BOAT!

"Father's Name" (5th Prize-Joke by Martin Talon)

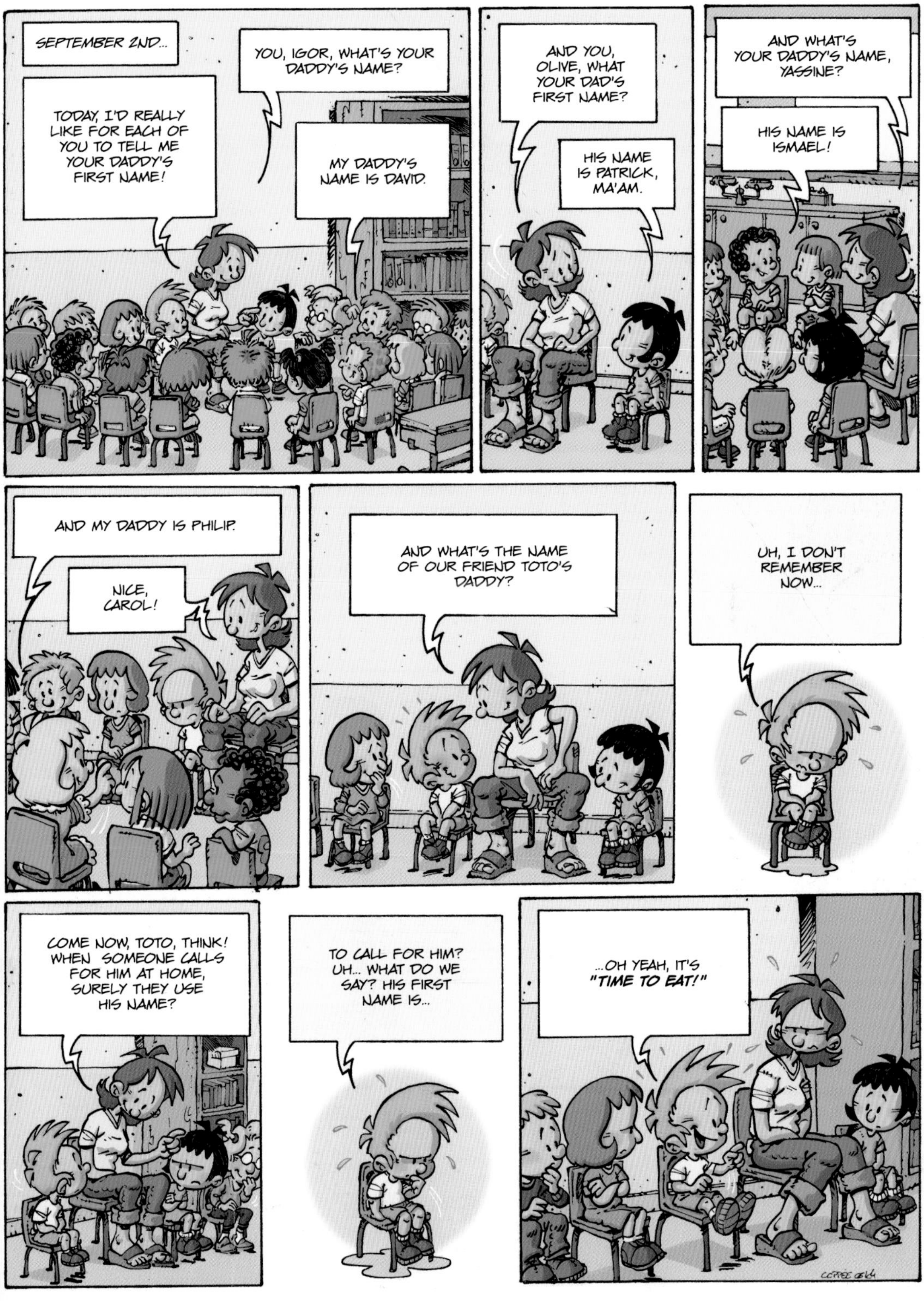

SEPTEMBER 2ND...
TODAY, I'D REALLY LIKE FOR EACH OF YOU TO TELL ME YOUR DADDY'S FIRST NAME!
YOU, IGOR, WHAT'S YOUR DADDY'S NAME?
MY DADDY'S NAME IS DAVID.
AND YOU, OLIVE, WHAT YOUR DAD'S FIRST NAME?
HIS NAME IS PATRICK, MA'AM.
AND WHAT'S YOUR DADDY'S NAME, YASSINE?
HIS NAME IS ISMAEL!
AND MY DADDY IS PHILIP.
NICE, CAROL!
AND WHAT'S THE NAME OF OUR FRIEND TOTO'S DADDY?
UH, I DON'T REMEMBER NOW...
COME NOW, TOTO, THINK! WHEN SOMEONE CALLS FOR HIM AT HOME, SURELY THEY USE HIS NAME?
TO CALL FOR HIM? UH... WHAT DO WE SAY? HIS FIRST NAME IS...
...OH YEAH, IT'S "TIME TO EAT!"

"A Memory Trick"

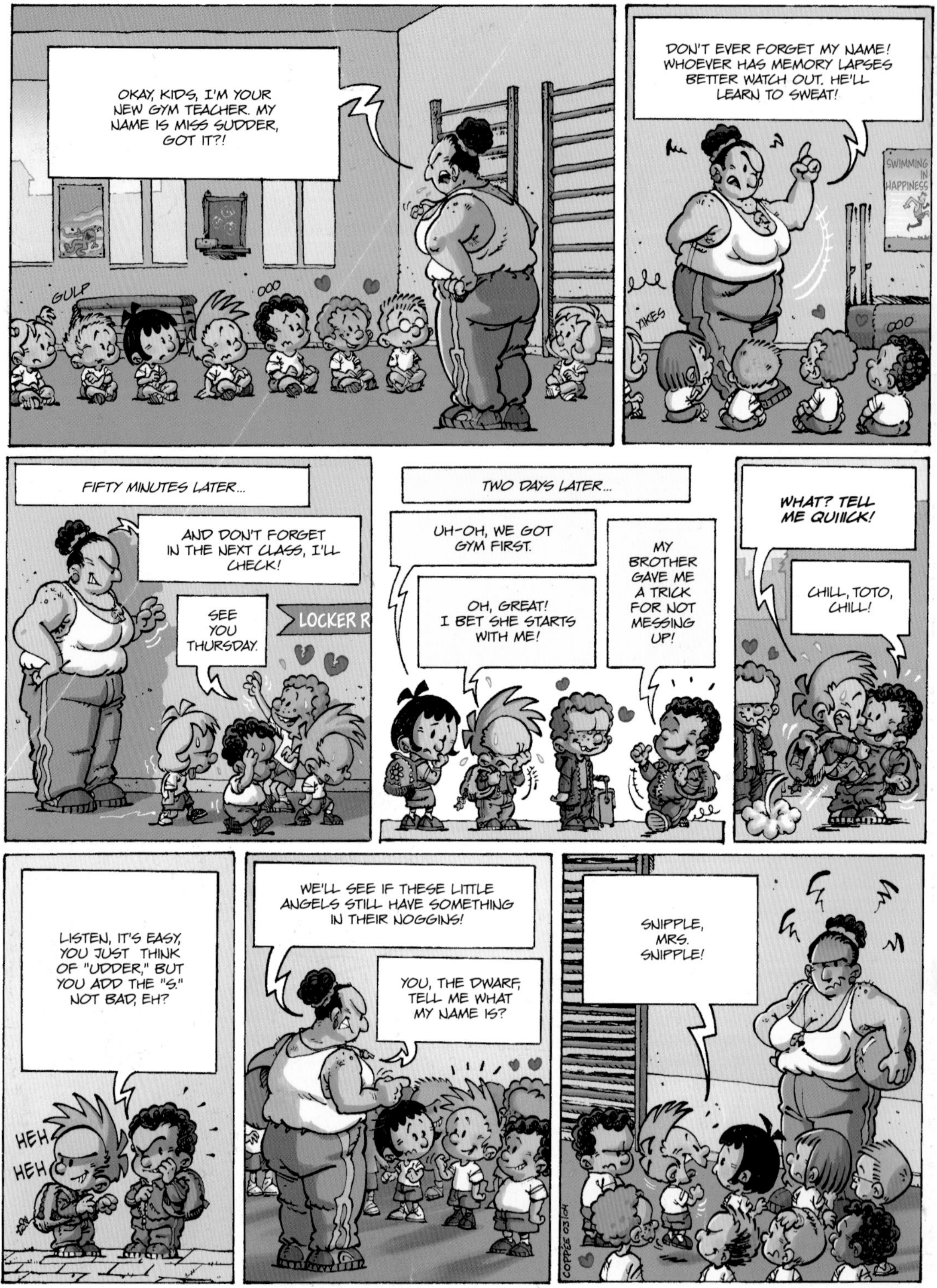

OKAY, KIDS, I'M YOUR NEW GYM TEACHER. MY NAME IS MISS SUDDER, GOT IT?!
GULP
OOO
DON'T EVER FORGET MY NAME! WHOEVER HAS MEMORY LAPSES BETTER WATCH OUT. HE'LL LEARN TO SWEAT!
SWIMMING IN HAPPINESS
YIKES
OOO
FIFTY MINUTES LATER...
AND DON'T FORGET IN THE NEXT CLASS, I'LL CHECK!
SEE YOU THURSDAY.
LOCKER R
TWO DAYS LATER...
UH-OH, WE GOT GYM FIRST.
OH, GREAT! I BET SHE STARTS WITH ME!
MY BROTHER GAVE ME A TRICK FOR NOT MESSING UP!
WHAT? TELL ME QUIIICK!
CHILL, TOTO, CHILL!
LISTEN, IT'S EASY, YOU JUST THINK OF "UDDER," BUT YOU ADD THE "S." NOT BAD, EH?
HEH HEH
WE'LL SEE IF THESE LITTLE ANGELS STILL HAVE SOMETHING IN THEIR NOGGINS!
YOU, THE DWARF, TELL ME WHAT MY NAME IS?
SNIPPLE, MRS. SNIPPLE!
COPPÉE 03/04

"Just Desserts"

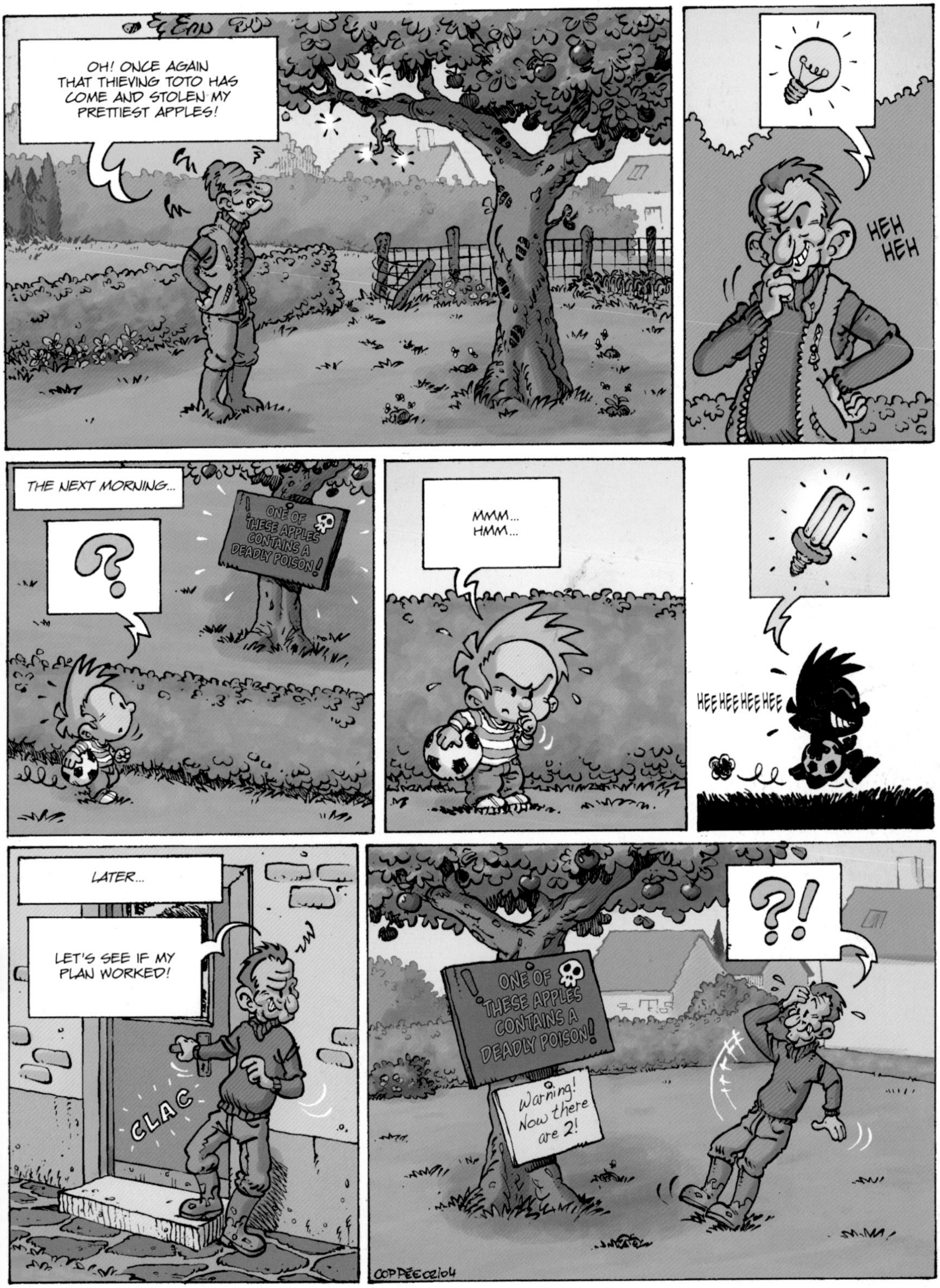
OH! ONCE AGAIN THAT THIEVING TOTO HAS COME AND STOLEN MY PRETTIEST APPLES!
HEH HEH
THE NEXT MORNING...
?
ONE OF THESE APPLES CONTAINS A DEADLY POISON!
MMM... HMM...
HEE HEE HEE HEE
LATER...
LET'S SEE IF MY PLAN WORKED!
CLAC
?!
ONE OF THESE APPLES CONTAINS A DEADLY POISON!
Warning! Now there are 2!
COPPÉE 02/04

"Who Knows Who It Is?"

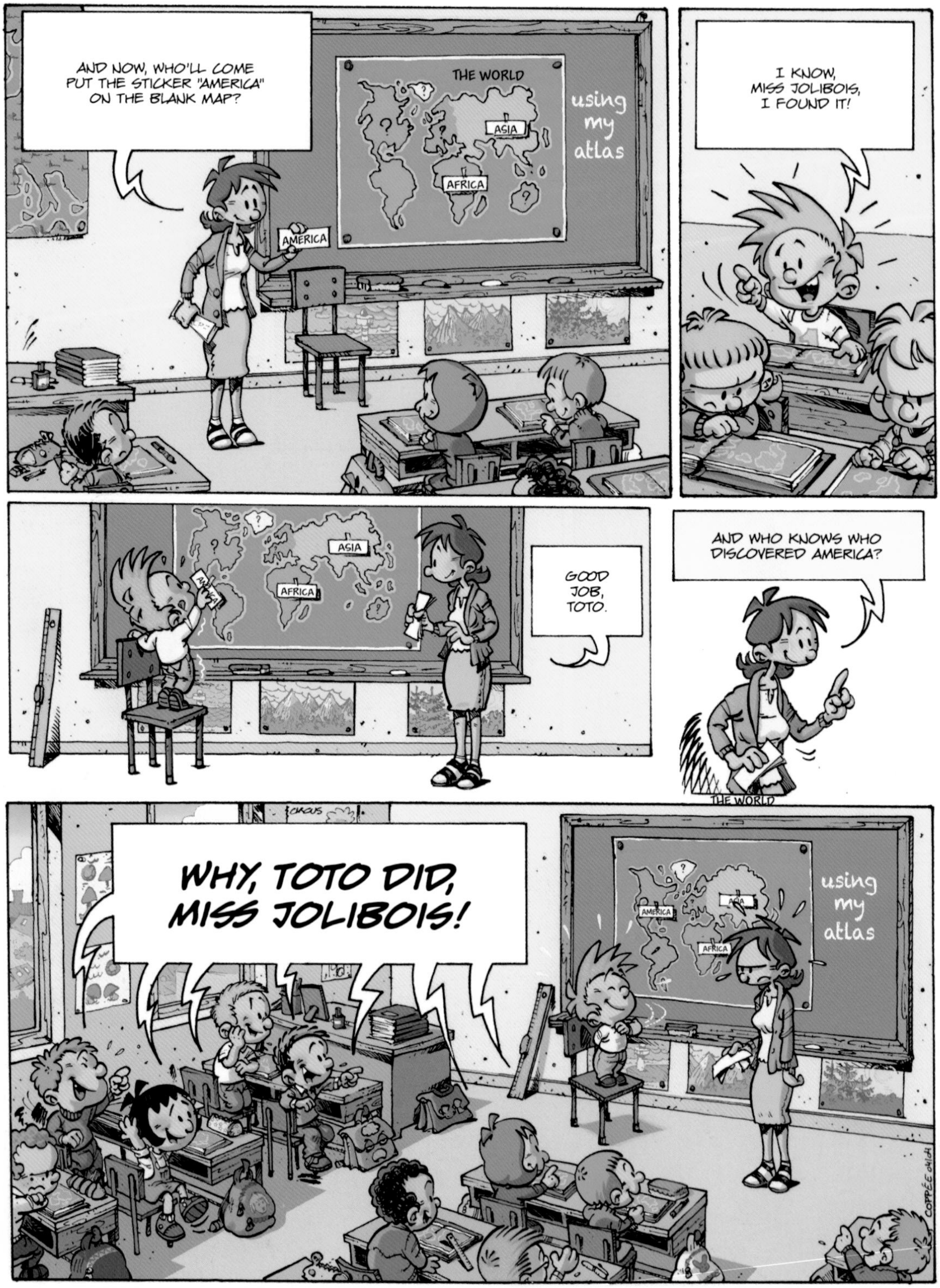
AND NOW, WHO'LL COME PUT THE STICKER "AMERICA" ON THE BLANK MAP?
THE WORLD
ASIA
AFRICA
AMERICA
using my atlas
I KNOW, MISS JOLIBOIS, I FOUND IT!
ASIA
AFRICA
GOOD JOB, TOTO.
AND WHO KNOWS WHO DISCOVERED AMERICA?
THE WORLD
WHY, TOTO DID, MISS JOLIBOIS!
AMERICA
ASIA
AFRICA
using my atlas

"A Piggish Dinner"

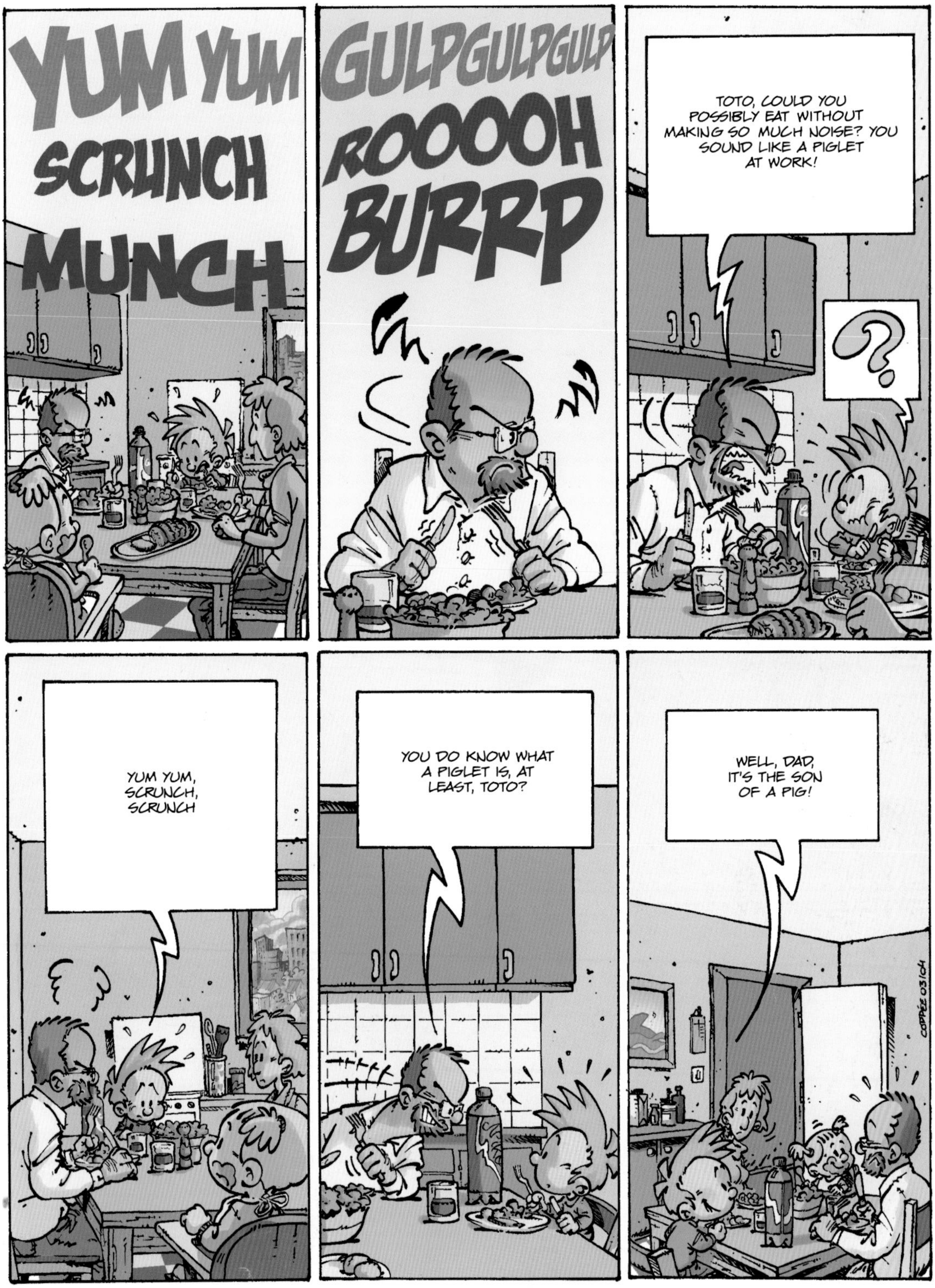

YUM YUM
SCRUNCH
MUNCH
GULPGULPGULP
ROOOOH
BURRP
TOTO, COULD YOU POSSIBLY EAT WITHOUT MAKING SO MUCH NOISE? YOU SOUND LIKE A PIGLET AT WORK!
?
YUM YUM, SCRUNCH, SCRUNCH
YOU DO KNOW WHAT A PIGLET IS, AT LEAST, TOTO?
WELL, DAD, IT'S THE SON OF A PIG!
COPPÉE 03/04

"A Genealogical Zoo"

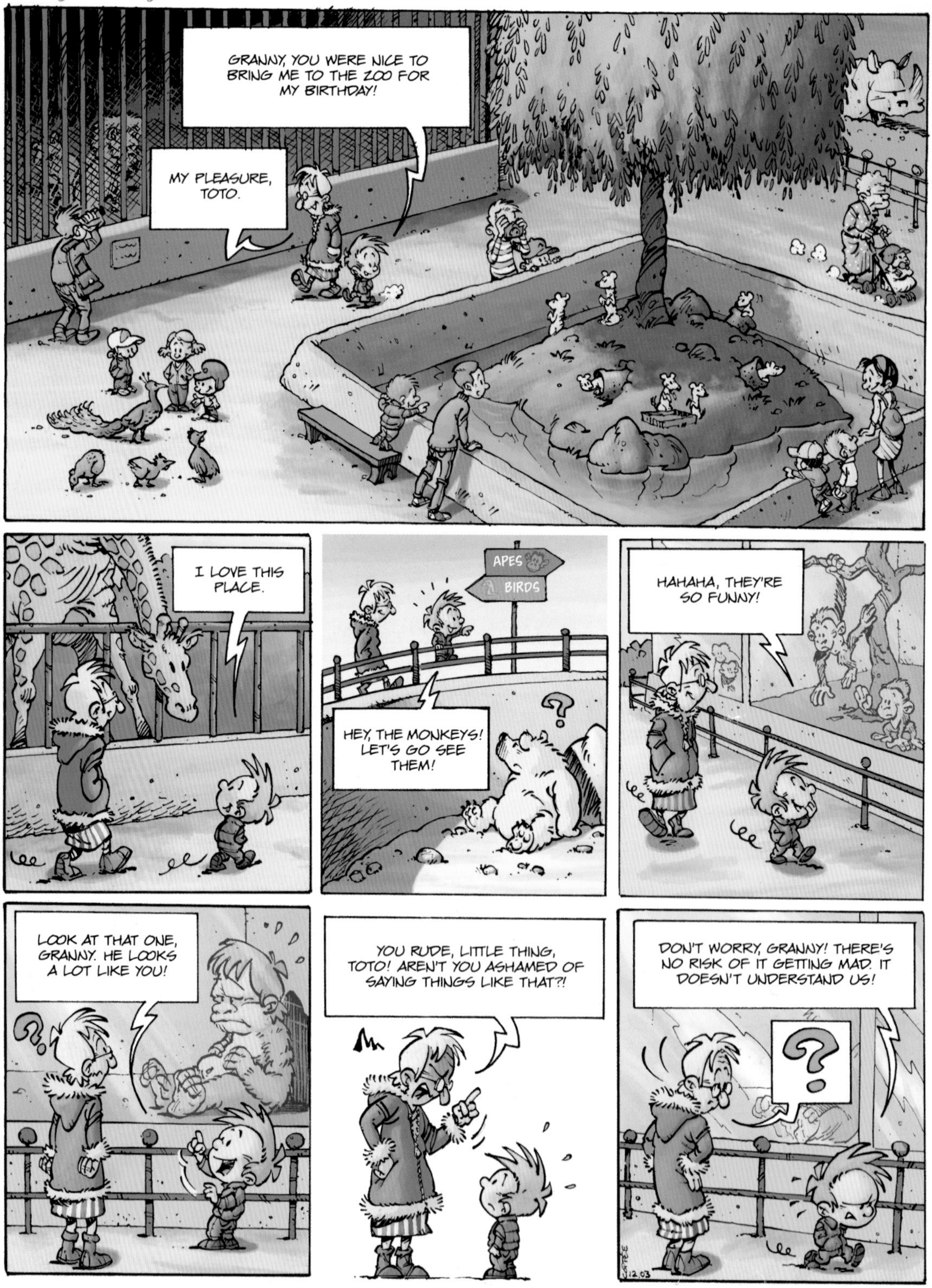
GRANNY, YOU WERE NICE TO BRING ME TO THE ZOO FOR MY BIRTHDAY!
MY PLEASURE, TOTO.
I LOVE THIS PLACE.
APES
BIRDS
HEY, THE MONKEYS! LET'S GO SEE THEM!
HAHAHA, THEY'RE SO FUNNY!
LOOK AT THAT ONE, GRANNY. HE LOOKS A LOT LIKE YOU!
YOU RUDE, LITTLE THING, TOTO! AREN'T YOU ASHAMED OF SAYING THINGS LIKE THAT?!
DON'T WORRY, GRANNY! THERE'S NO RISK OF IT GETTING MAD. IT DOESN'T UNDERSTAND US!
?

"A Stupid Discussion"

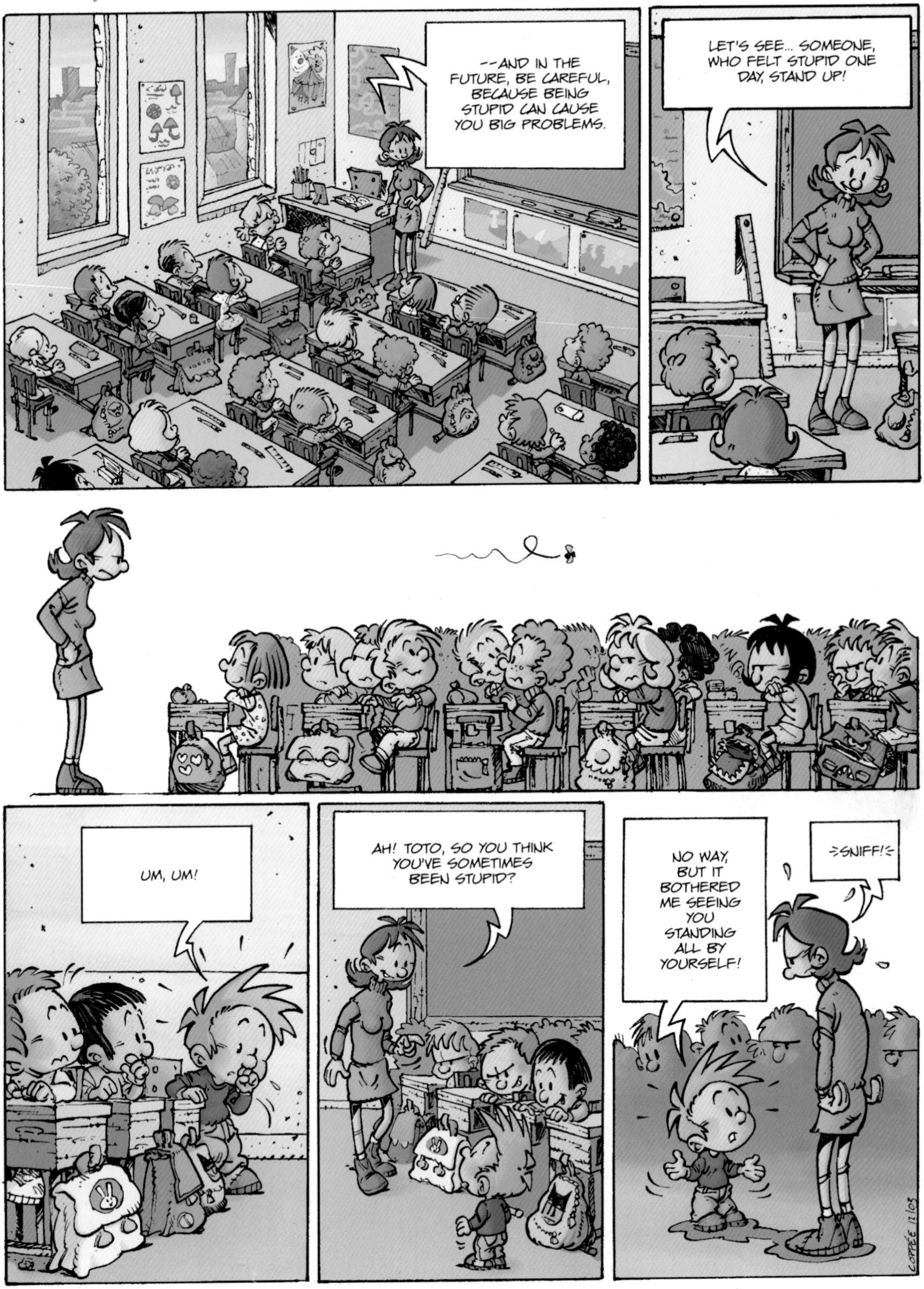
--AND IN THE FUTURE, BE CAREFUL, BECAUSE BEING STUPID CAN CAUSE YOU BIG PROBLEMS.
LET'S SEE... SOMEONE, WHO FELT STUPID ONE DAY, STAND UP!
UM, UM!
AH! TOTO, SO YOU THINK YOU'VE SOMETIMES BEEN STUPID?
NO WAY, BUT IT BOTHERED ME SEEING YOU STANDING ALL BY YOURSELF!
SNIFF!
COPPÉE 12/03

"False Hope"

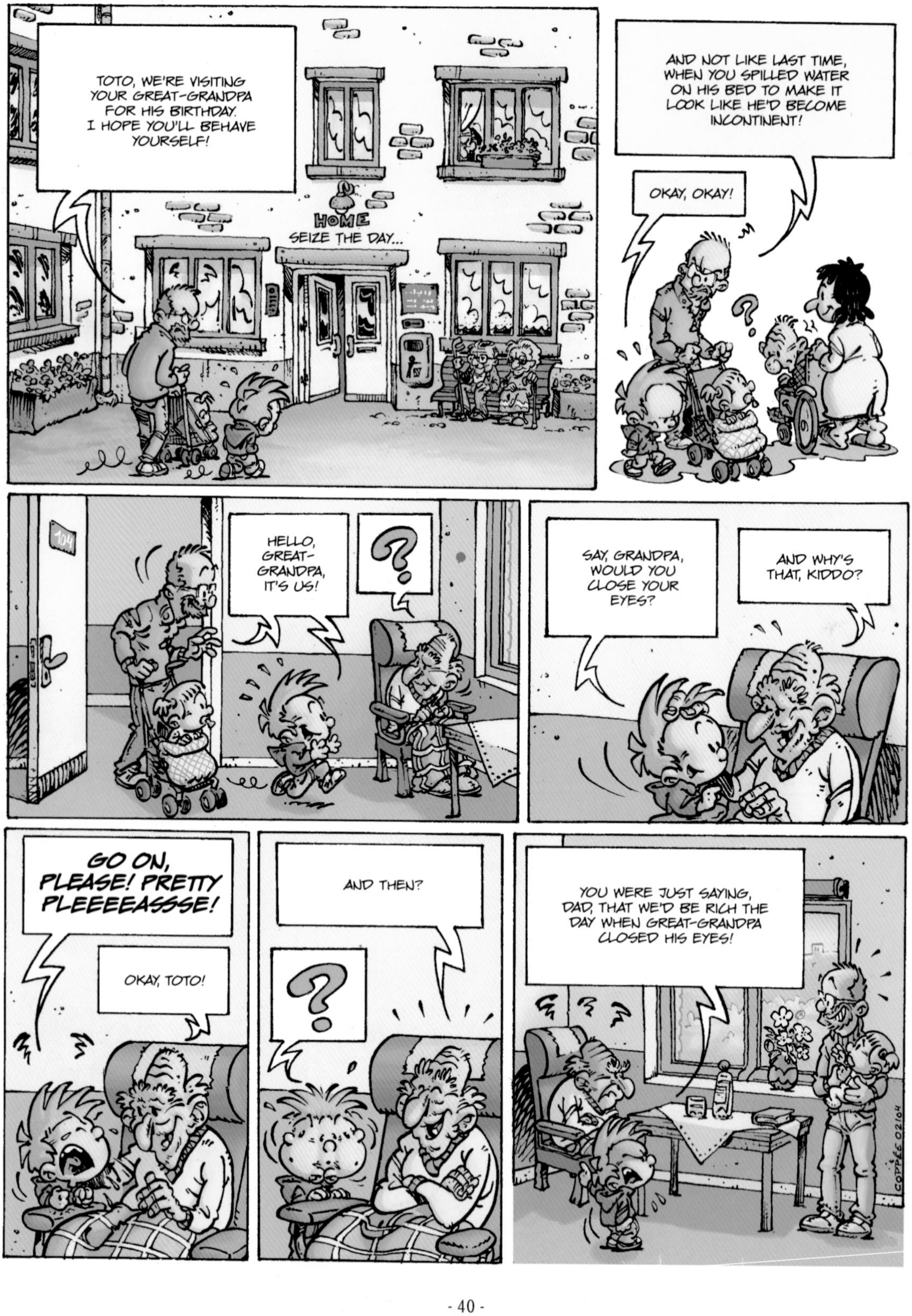
TOTO, WE'RE VISITING YOUR GREAT-GRANDPA FOR HIS BIRTHDAY. I HOPE YOU'LL BEHAVE YOURSELF!
HOME
SEIZE THE DAY...
AND NOT LIKE LAST TIME, WHEN YOU SPILLED WATER ON HIS BED TO MAKE IT LOOK LIKE HE'D BECOME INCONTINENT!
OKAY, OKAY!
104
HELLO, GREAT-GRANDPA, IT'S US!
?
SAY, GRANDPA, WOULD YOU CLOSE YOUR EYES?
AND WHY'S THAT, KIDDO?
GO ON, PLEASE! PRETTY PLEEEEASSSE!
OKAY, TOTO!
AND THEN?
?
YOU WERE JUST SAYING, DAD, THAT WE'D BE RICH THE DAY WHEN GREAT-GRANDPA CLOSED HIS EYES!
COPPÉE 02/04

"A Funny Fall"

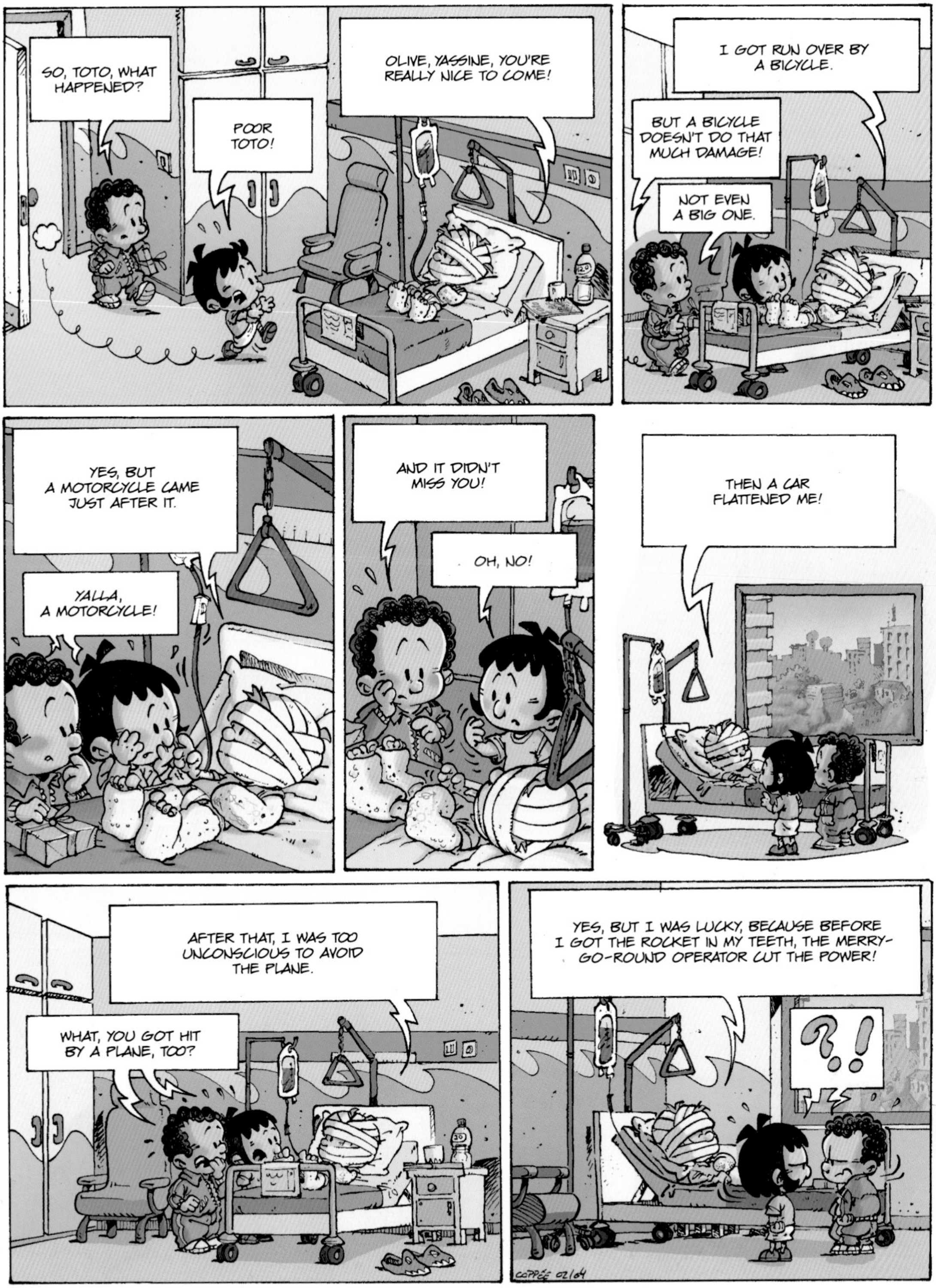
SO, TOTO, WHAT HAPPENED?
POOR TOTO!
OLIVE, YASSINE, YOU'RE REALLY NICE TO COME!
I GOT RUN OVER BY A BICYCLE.
BUT A BICYCLE DOESN'T DO THAT MUCH DAMAGE!
NOT EVEN A BIG ONE.
YES, BUT A MOTORCYCLE CAME JUST AFTER IT.
YALLA, A MOTORCYCLE!
AND IT DIDN'T MISS YOU!
OH, NO!
THEN A CAR FLATTENED ME!
AFTER THAT, I WAS TOO UNCONSCIOUS TO AVOID THE PLANE.
WHAT, YOU GOT HIT BY A PLANE, TOO?
YES, BUT I WAS LUCKY, BECAUSE BEFORE I GOT THE ROCKET IN MY TEETH, THE MERRY-GO-ROUND OPERATOR CUT THE POWER!
?!
COPPÉE 02/04

"Slow Times"

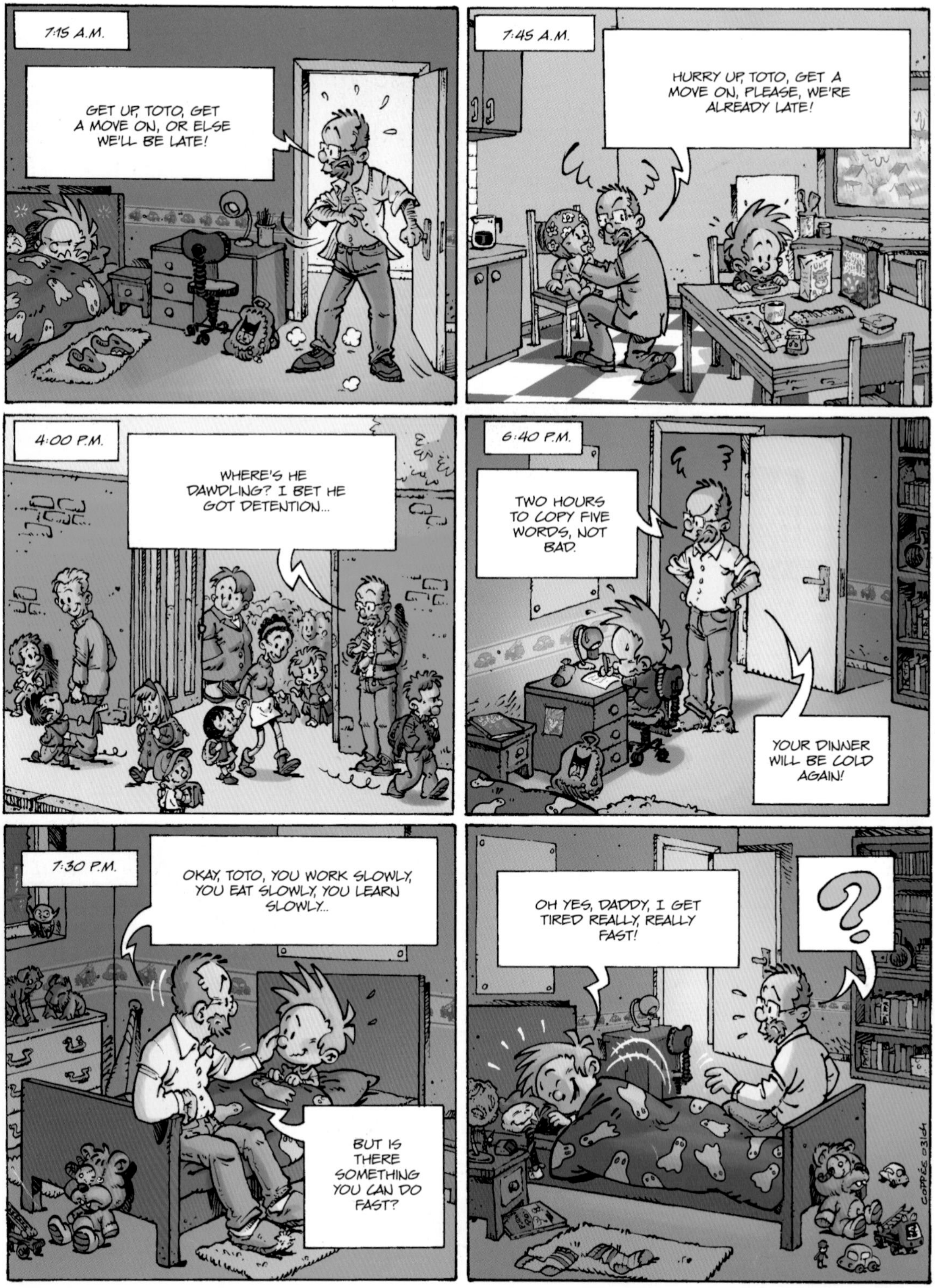
7:15 A.M.
GET UP, TOTO, GET A MOVE ON, OR ELSE WE'LL BE LATE!
7:45 A.M.
HURRY UP, TOTO, GET A MOVE ON, PLEASE, WE'RE ALREADY LATE!
4:00 P.M.
WHERE'S HE DAWDLING? I BET HE GOT DETENTION...
6:40 P.M.
TWO HOURS TO COPY FIVE WORDS, NOT BAD.
YOUR DINNER WILL BE COLD AGAIN!
7:30 P.M.
OKAY, TOTO, YOU WORK SLOWLY, YOU EAT SLOWLY, YOU LEARN SLOWLY...
BUT IS THERE SOMETHING YOU CAN DO FAST?
OH YES, DADDY, I GET TIRED REALLY, REALLY FAST!
?

"The Fruit of Fractions"

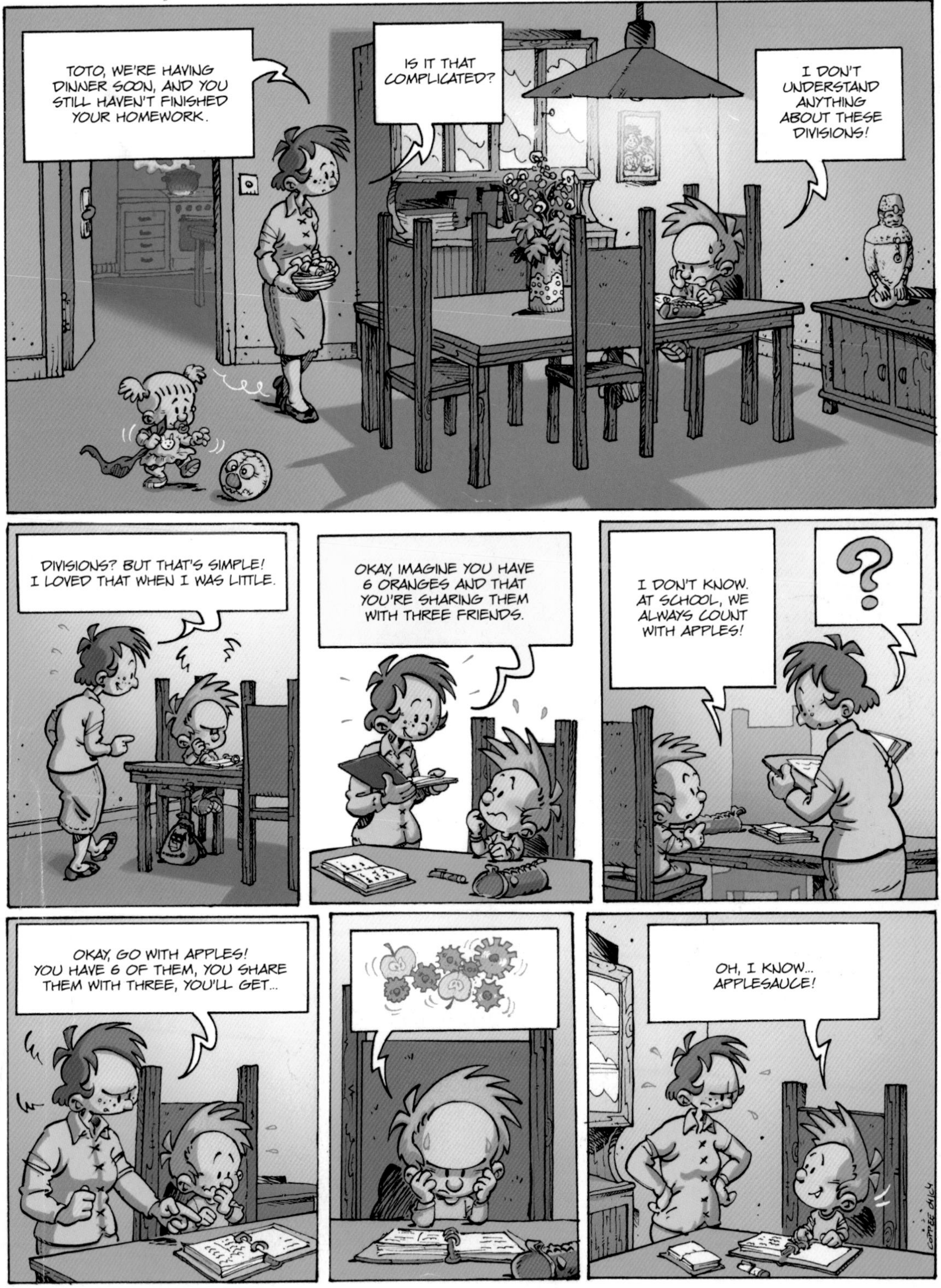
TOTO, WE'RE HAVING DINNER SOON, AND YOU STILL HAVEN'T FINISHED YOUR HOMEWORK.
IS IT THAT COMPLICATED?
I DON'T UNDERSTAND ANYTHING ABOUT THESE DIVISIONS!
DIVISIONS? BUT THAT'S SIMPLE! I LOVED THAT WHEN I WAS LITTLE.
OKAY, IMAGINE YOU HAVE 6 ORANGES AND THAT YOU'RE SHARING THEM WITH THREE FRIENDS.
I DON'T KNOW. AT SCHOOL, WE ALWAYS COUNT WITH APPLES!
?
OKAY, GO WITH APPLES! YOU HAVE 6 OF THEM, YOU SHARE THEM WITH THREE, YOU'LL GET...
OH, I KNOW... APPLESAUCE!

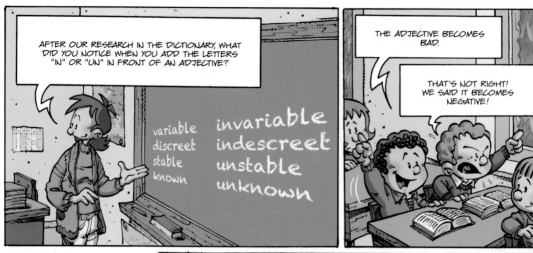

AFTER OUR RESEARCH IN THE DICTIONARY, WHAT DID YOU NOTICE WHEN YOU ADD THE LETTERS "IN" OR "UN" IN FRONT OF AN ADJECTIVE?

variable invariable
discreet indescreet
stable   unstable
known   unknown

THE ADJECTIVE BECOMES BAD.

THAT'S NOT RIGHT! WE SAID IT BECOMES NEGATIVE!

GOOD, IGOR!

GIVE ME SOME WORDS STARTING WITH "IN" OR "UN" THAT HAVE A NEGATIVE MEANING!

INVISIBLE!

INVOLUNTARY!

INCOMPLETE!

UNSATISFIED!

UNFAITHFUL!

perimeter
circl
square
2 x (3+H)

PREHISTORY

ME, ME, I GOT ONE!

WELL, WE'RE LISTENING, TOTO!

INSTRUCTOR!

COPPÉE 07/04

"Christmas Gift"

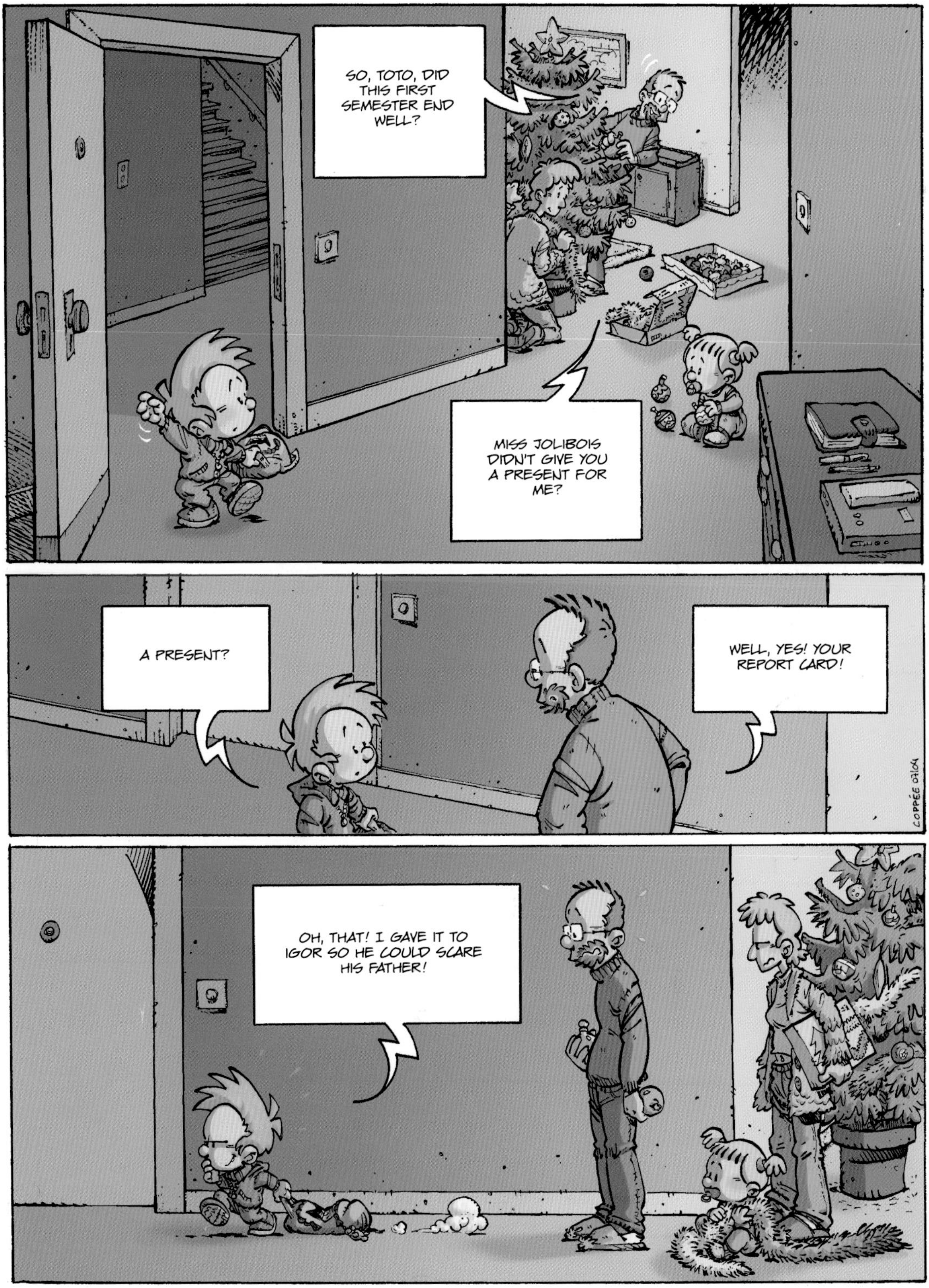
SO, TOTO, DID THIS FIRST SEMESTER END WELL?
MISS JOLIBOIS DIDN'T GIVE YOU A PRESENT FOR ME?
A PRESENT?
WELL, YES! YOUR REPORT CARD!
COPPÉE 07/04
OH, THAT! I GAVE IT TO IGOR SO HE COULD SCARE HIS FATHER!

"A Ticket for Her" (2nd Prize-Joke by Jeanne Baliteau)

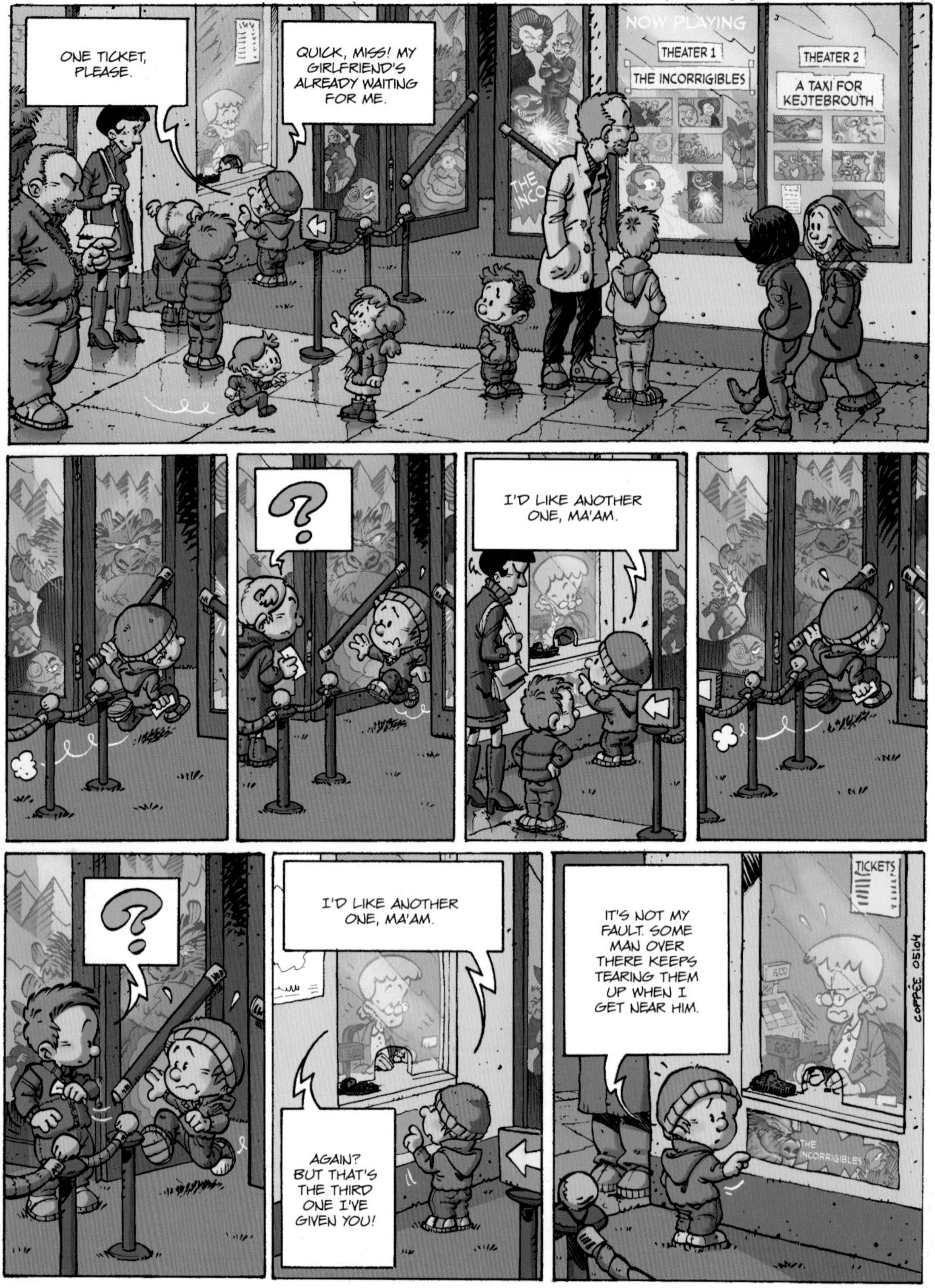

ONE TICKET, PLEASE.
QUICK, MISS! MY GIRLFRIEND'S ALREADY WAITING FOR ME.
NOW PLAYING
THEATER 1
THE INCORRIGIBLES
THEATER 2
A TAXI FOR KEJTEBROUTH
?
I'D LIKE ANOTHER ONE, MA'AM.
?
I'D LIKE ANOTHER ONE, MA'AM.
AGAIN? BUT THAT'S THE THIRD ONE I'VE GIVEN YOU!
IT'S NOT MY FAULT. SOME MAN OVER THERE KEEPS TEARING THEM UP WHEN I GET NEAR HIM.
TICKETS
THE INCORRIGIBLES
COPPÉE 05104

"Original Origins"

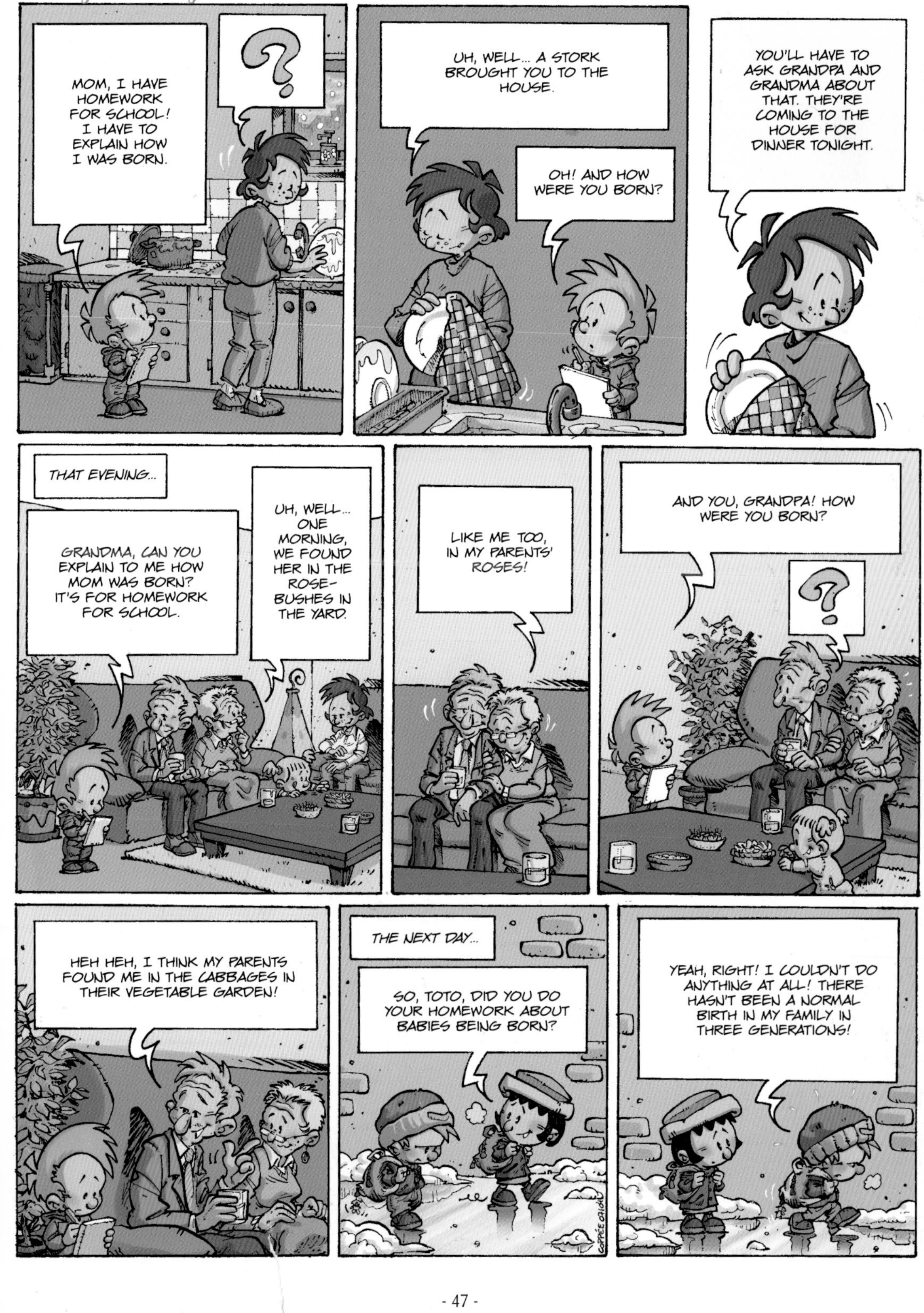

MOM, I HAVE HOMEWORK FOR SCHOOL! I HAVE TO EXPLAIN HOW I WAS BORN.
?
UH, WELL... A STORK BROUGHT YOU TO THE HOUSE.
OH! AND HOW WERE YOU BORN?
YOU'LL HAVE TO ASK GRANDPA AND GRANDMA ABOUT THAT. THEY'RE COMING TO THE HOUSE FOR DINNER TONIGHT.
THAT EVENING...
GRANDMA, CAN YOU EXPLAIN TO ME HOW MOM WAS BORN? IT'S FOR HOMEWORK FOR SCHOOL.
UH, WELL... ONE MORNING, WE FOUND HER IN THE ROSE-BUSHES IN THE YARD.
LIKE ME TOO, IN MY PARENTS' ROSES!
AND YOU, GRANDPA! HOW WERE YOU BORN?
?
HEH HEH, I THINK MY PARENTS FOUND ME IN THE CABBAGES IN THEIR VEGETABLE GARDEN!
THE NEXT DAY...
SO, TOTO, DID YOU DO YOUR HOMEWORK ABOUT BABIES BEING BORN?
YEAH, RIGHT! I COULDN'T DO ANYTHING AT ALL! THERE HASN'T BEEN A NORMAL BIRTH IN MY FAMILY IN THREE GENERATIONS!

"Circumwhat"

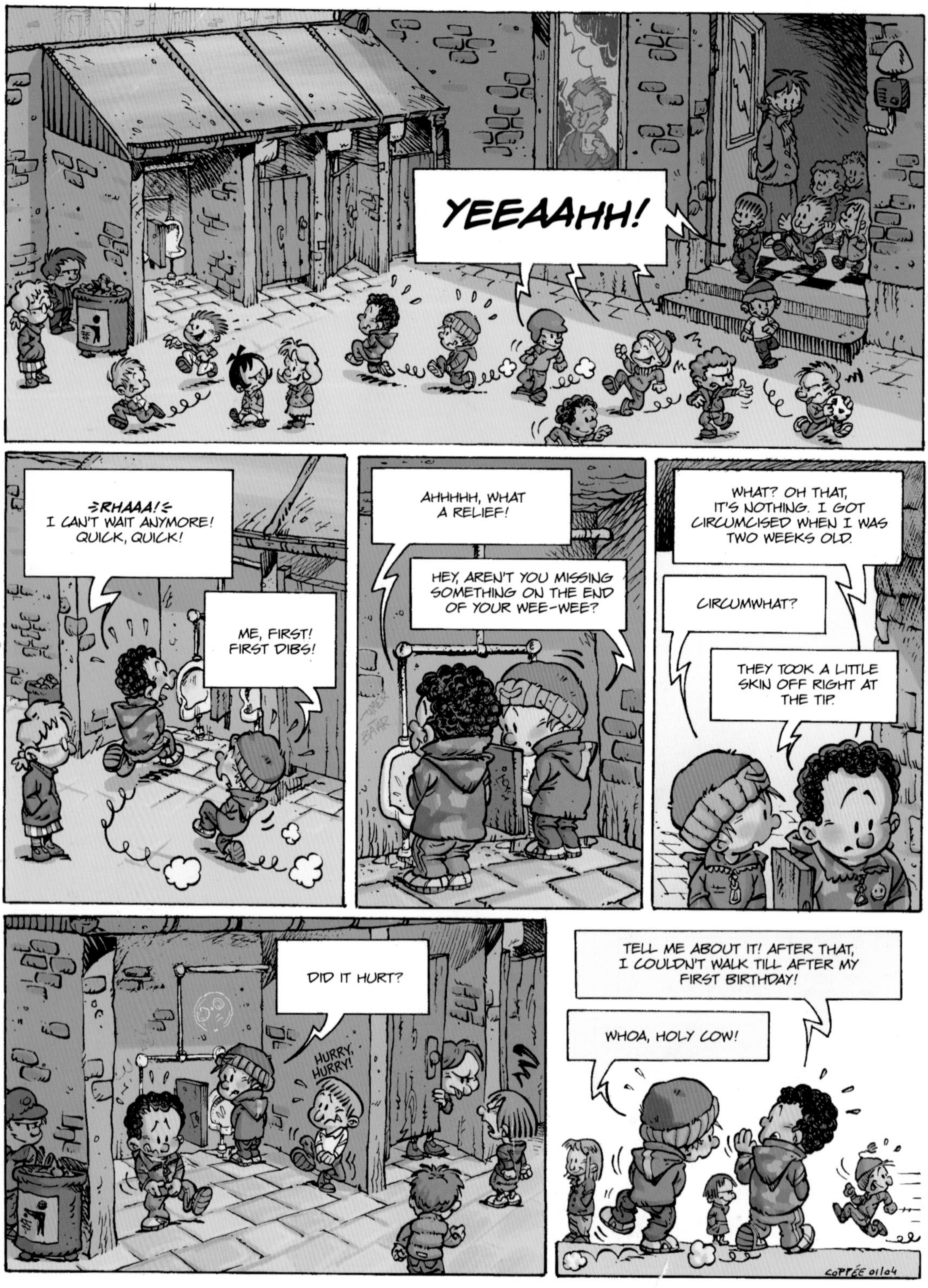
YEEAAHH!
RHAAA!
I CAN'T WAIT ANYMORE! QUICK, QUICK!
ME, FIRST! FIRST DIBS!
AHHHHH, WHAT A RELIEF!
HEY, AREN'T YOU MISSING SOMETHING ON THE END OF YOUR WEE-WEE?
WHAT? OH THAT, IT'S NOTHING. I GOT CIRCUMCISED WHEN I WAS TWO WEEKS OLD.
CIRCUMWHAT?
THEY TOOK A LITTLE SKIN OFF RIGHT AT THE TIP.
DID IT HURT?
HURRY, HURRY!
TELL ME ABOUT IT! AFTER THAT, I COULDN'T WALK TILL AFTER MY FIRST BIRTHDAY!
WHOA, HOLY COW!
COPPÉE 01/04

"Rhyming Games"

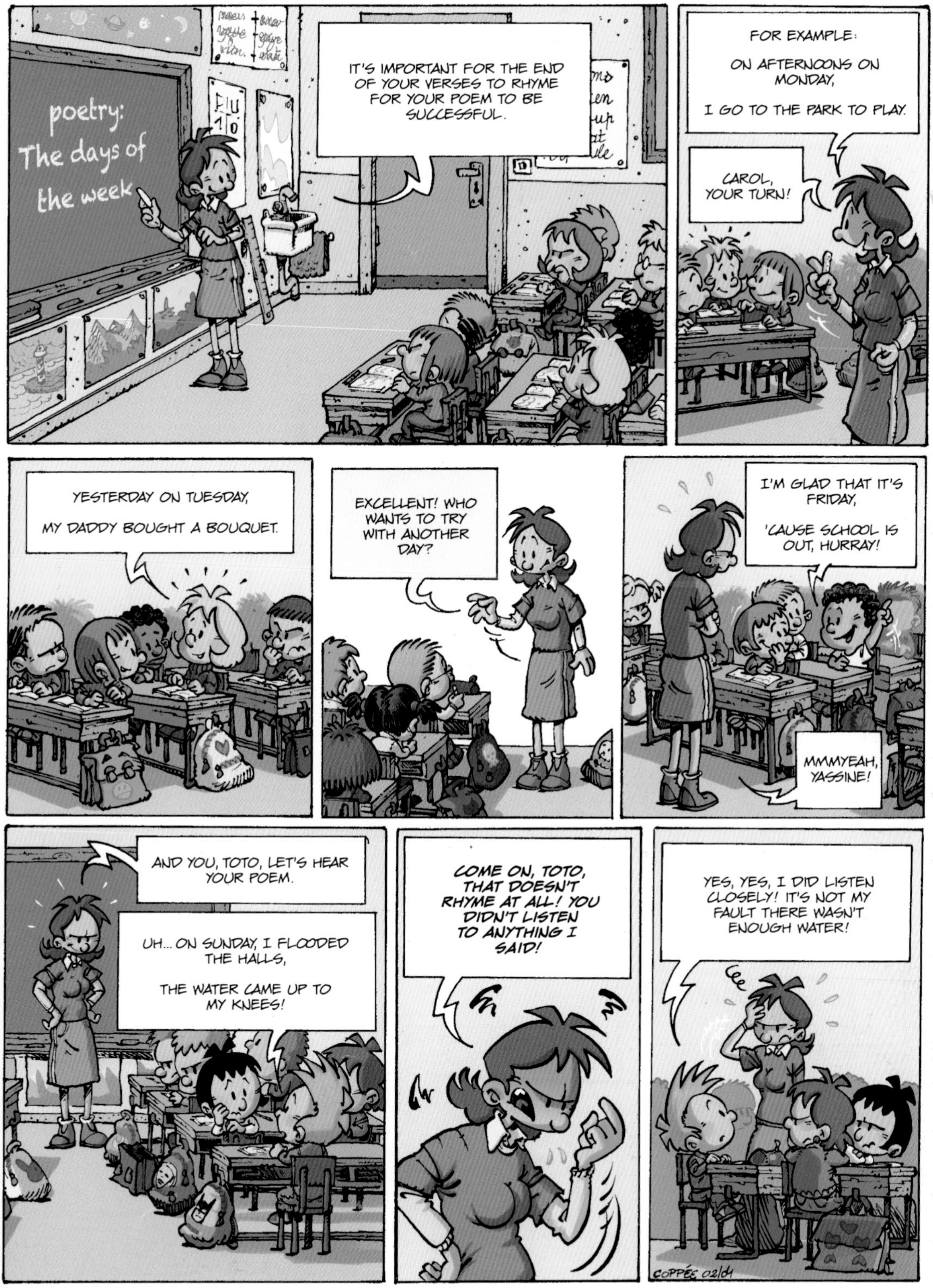
poetry: The days of the week
IT'S IMPORTANT FOR THE END OF YOUR VERSES TO RHYME FOR YOUR POEM TO BE SUCCESSFUL.
FOR EXAMPLE:
ON AFTERNOONS ON MONDAY,
I GO TO THE PARK TO PLAY.
CAROL, YOUR TURN!
YESTERDAY ON TUESDAY,
MY DADDY BOUGHT A BOUQUET.
EXCELLENT! WHO WANTS TO TRY WITH ANOTHER DAY?
I'M GLAD THAT IT'S FRIDAY,
'CAUSE SCHOOL IS OUT, HURRAY!
MMMYEAH, YASSINE!
AND YOU, TOTO, LET'S HEAR YOUR POEM.
UH... ON SUNDAY, I FLOODED THE HALLS,
THE WATER CAME UP TO MY KNEES!
COME ON, TOTO, THAT DOESN'T RHYME AT ALL! YOU DIDN'T LISTEN TO ANYTHING I SAID!
YES, YES, I DID LISTEN CLOSELY! IT'S NOT MY FAULT THERE WASN'T ENOUGH WATER!
COPPÉE 02/01

"Anxiety"

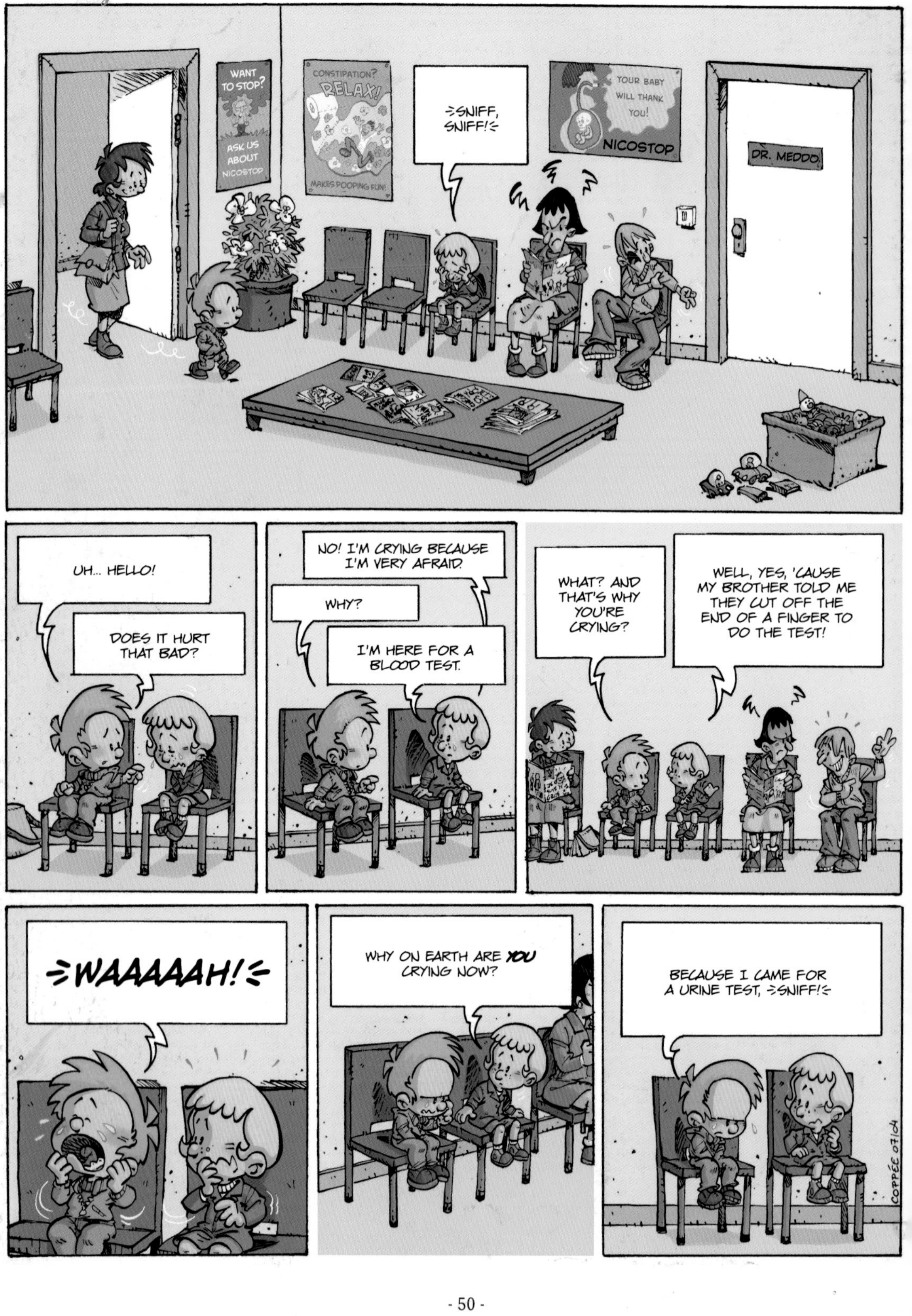

WANT TO STOP?
ASK US ABOUT NICOSTOP
CONSTIPATION?
RELAX!
MAKES POOPING FUN!
=SNIFF, SNIFF!=
YOUR BABY WILL THANK YOU!
NICOSTOP
DR. MEDDO
UH... HELLO!
DOES IT HURT THAT BAD?
NO! I'M CRYING BECAUSE I'M VERY AFRAID.
WHY?
I'M HERE FOR A BLOOD TEST.
WHAT? AND THAT'S WHY YOU'RE CRYING?
WELL, YES, 'CAUSE MY BROTHER TOLD ME THEY CUT OFF THE END OF A FINGER TO DO THE TEST!
=WAAAAAH!=
WHY ON EARTH ARE **YOU** CRYING NOW?
BECAUSE I CAME FOR A URINE TEST, =SNIFF!=
COPPÉE 07/04

"As Easy as Pie" (4th Prize-Joke by Floriane Joveneau)

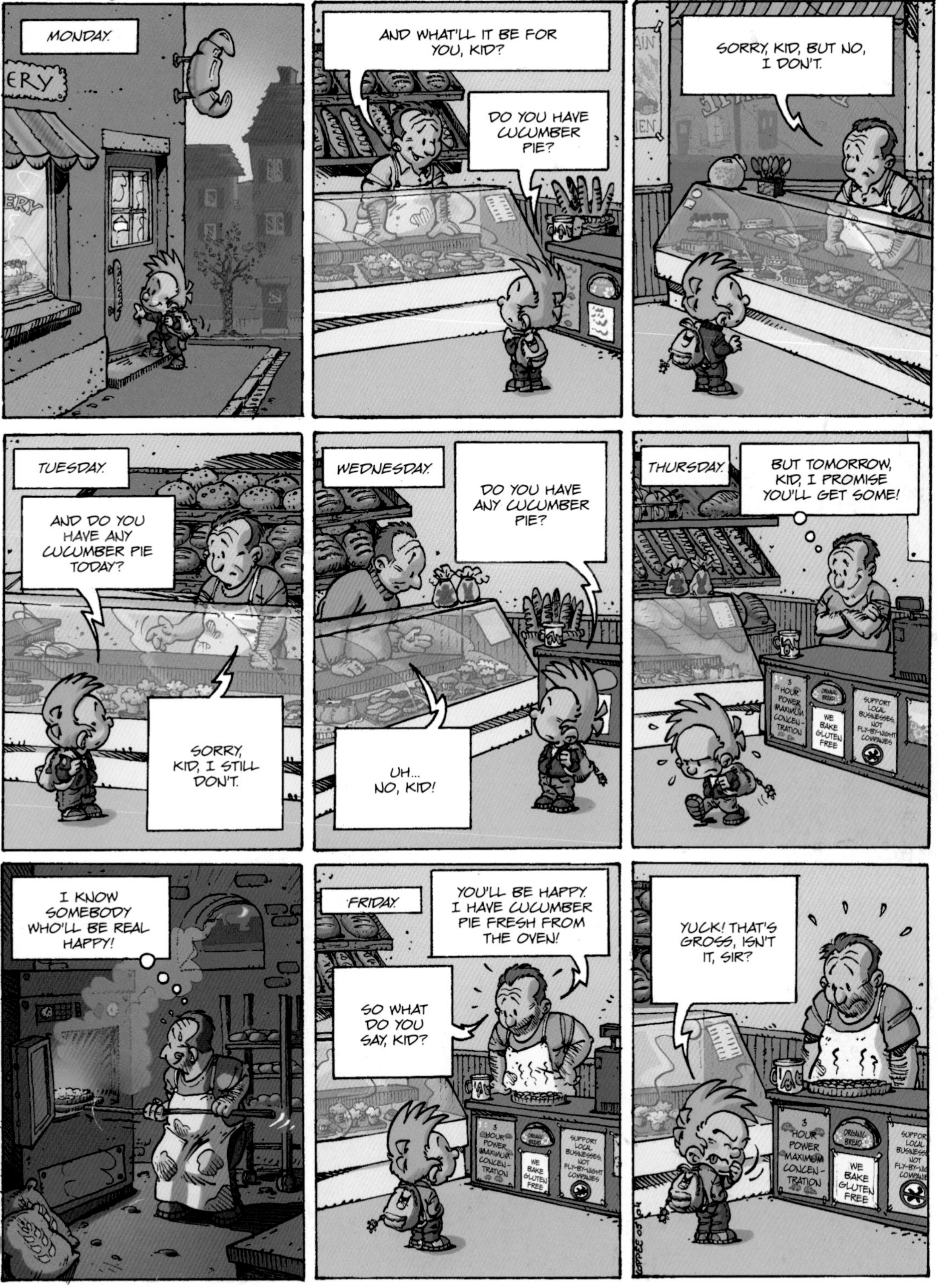

MONDAY.
ERY
AND WHAT'LL IT BE FOR YOU, KID?
DO YOU HAVE CUCUMBER PIE?
SORRY, KID, BUT NO, I DON'T.
TUESDAY.
AND DO YOU HAVE ANY CUCUMBER PIE TODAY?
SORRY, KID, I STILL DON'T.
WEDNESDAY.
DO YOU HAVE ANY CUCUMBER PIE?
UH... NO, KID!
THURSDAY.
BUT TOMORROW, KID, I PROMISE YOU'LL GET SOME!
3 HOUR POWER MAXIMUM CONCENTRATION
ORGANIC BREAD
WE BAKE GLUTEN FREE
SUPPORT LOCAL BUSINESSES, NOT FLY-BY-NIGHT COMPANIES
I KNOW SOMEBODY WHO'LL BE REAL HAPPY!
FRIDAY.
YOU'LL BE HAPPY. I HAVE CUCUMBER PIE FRESH FROM THE OVEN!
SO WHAT DO YOU SAY, KID?
YUCK! THAT'S GROSS, ISN'T IT, SIR?

"That Old Stranger"

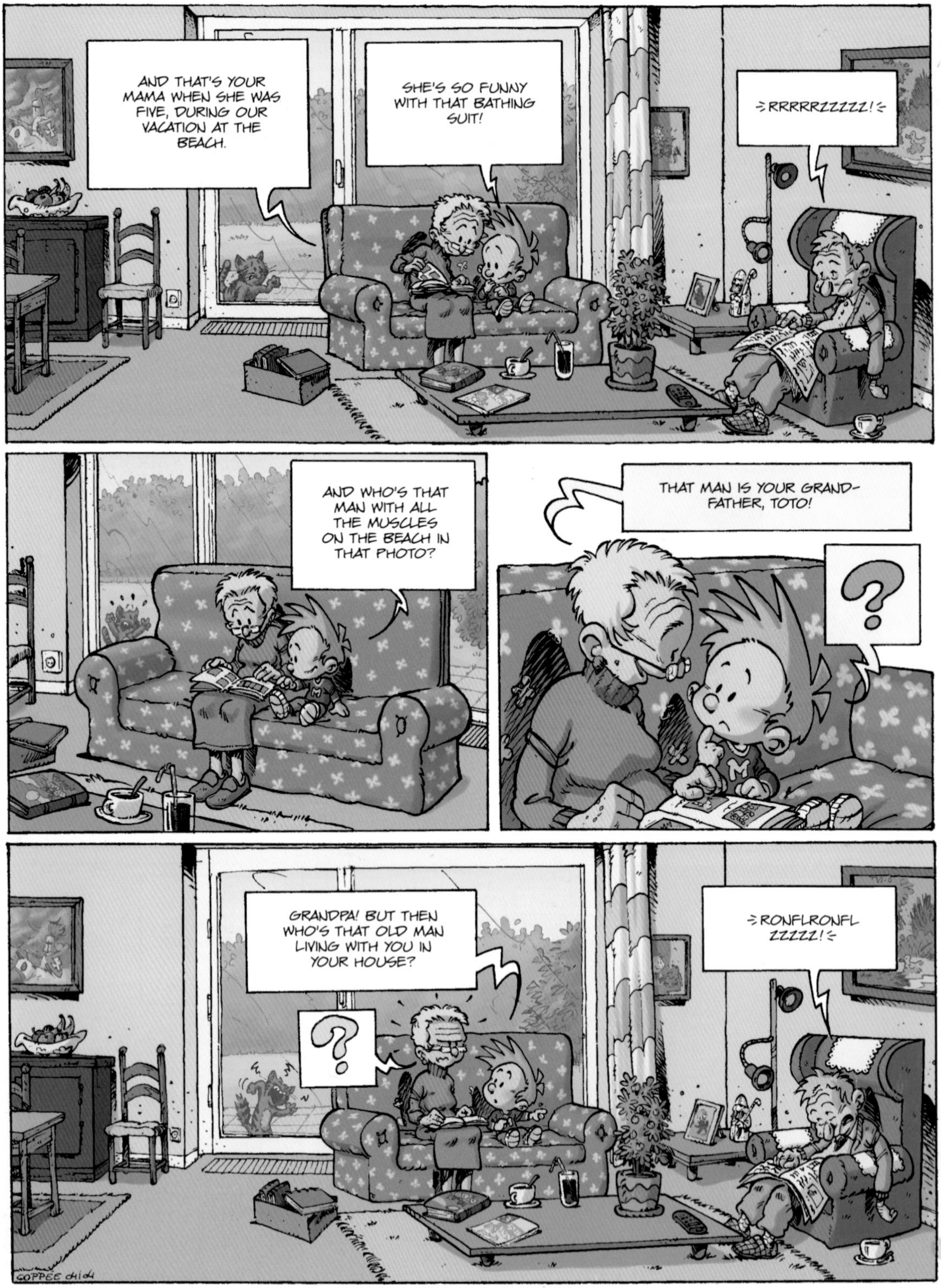
AND THAT'S YOUR MAMA WHEN SHE WAS FIVE, DURING OUR VACATION AT THE BEACH.
SHE'S SO FUNNY WITH THAT BATHING SUIT!
RRRRRZZZZZ!
AND WHO'S THAT MAN WITH ALL THE MUSCLES ON THE BEACH IN THAT PHOTO?
THAT MAN IS YOUR GRAND-FATHER, TOTO!
?
GRANDPA! BUT THEN WHO'S THAT OLD MAN LIVING WITH YOU IN YOUR HOUSE?
?
RONFLRONFL ZZZZZ!
GOPPEE

"Sacred Cows"

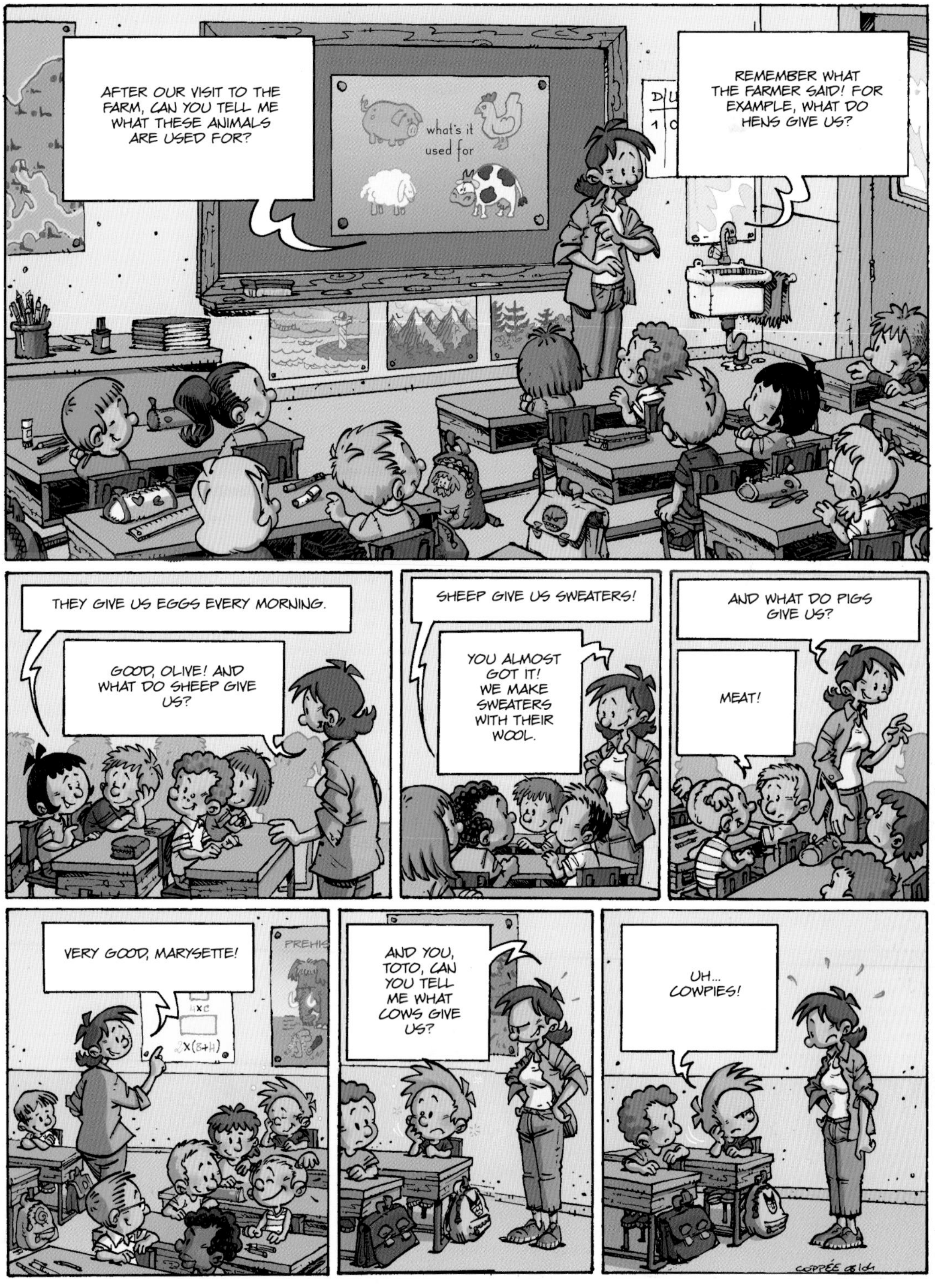
AFTER OUR VISIT TO THE FARM, CAN YOU TELL ME WHAT THESE ANIMALS ARE USED FOR?
what's it used for
REMEMBER WHAT THE FARMER SAID! FOR EXAMPLE, WHAT DO HENS GIVE US?
THEY GIVE US EGGS EVERY MORNING.
GOOD, OLIVE! AND WHAT DO SHEEP GIVE US?
SHEEP GIVE US SWEATERS!
YOU ALMOST GOT IT! WE MAKE SWEATERS WITH THEIR WOOL.
AND WHAT DO PIGS GIVE US?
MEAT!
VERY GOOD, MARYSETTE!
AND YOU, TOTO, CAN YOU TELL ME WHAT COWS GIVE US?
UH... COWPIES!

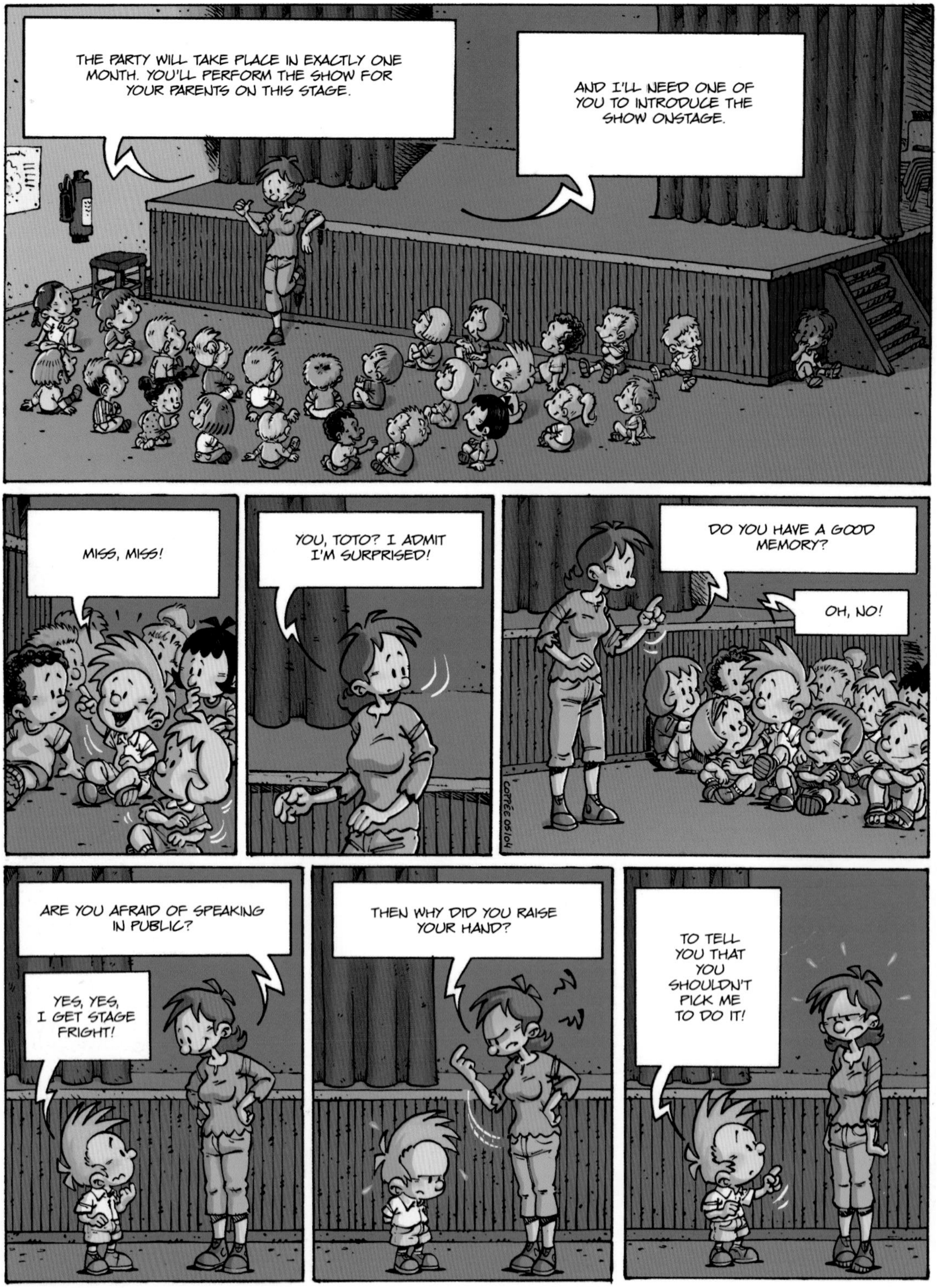
THE PARTY WILL TAKE PLACE IN EXACTLY ONE MONTH. YOU'LL PERFORM THE SHOW FOR YOUR PARENTS ON THIS STAGE.
AND I'LL NEED ONE OF YOU TO INTRODUCE THE SHOW ONSTAGE.
MISS, MISS!
YOU, TOTO? I ADMIT I'M SURPRISED!
DO YOU HAVE A GOOD MEMORY?
OH, NO!
ARE YOU AFRAID OF SPEAKING IN PUBLIC?
YES, YES, I GET STAGE FRIGHT!
THEN WHY DID YOU RAISE YOUR HAND?
TO TELL YOU THAT YOU SHOULDN'T PICK ME TO DO IT!

"H2 Uh-Oh!"

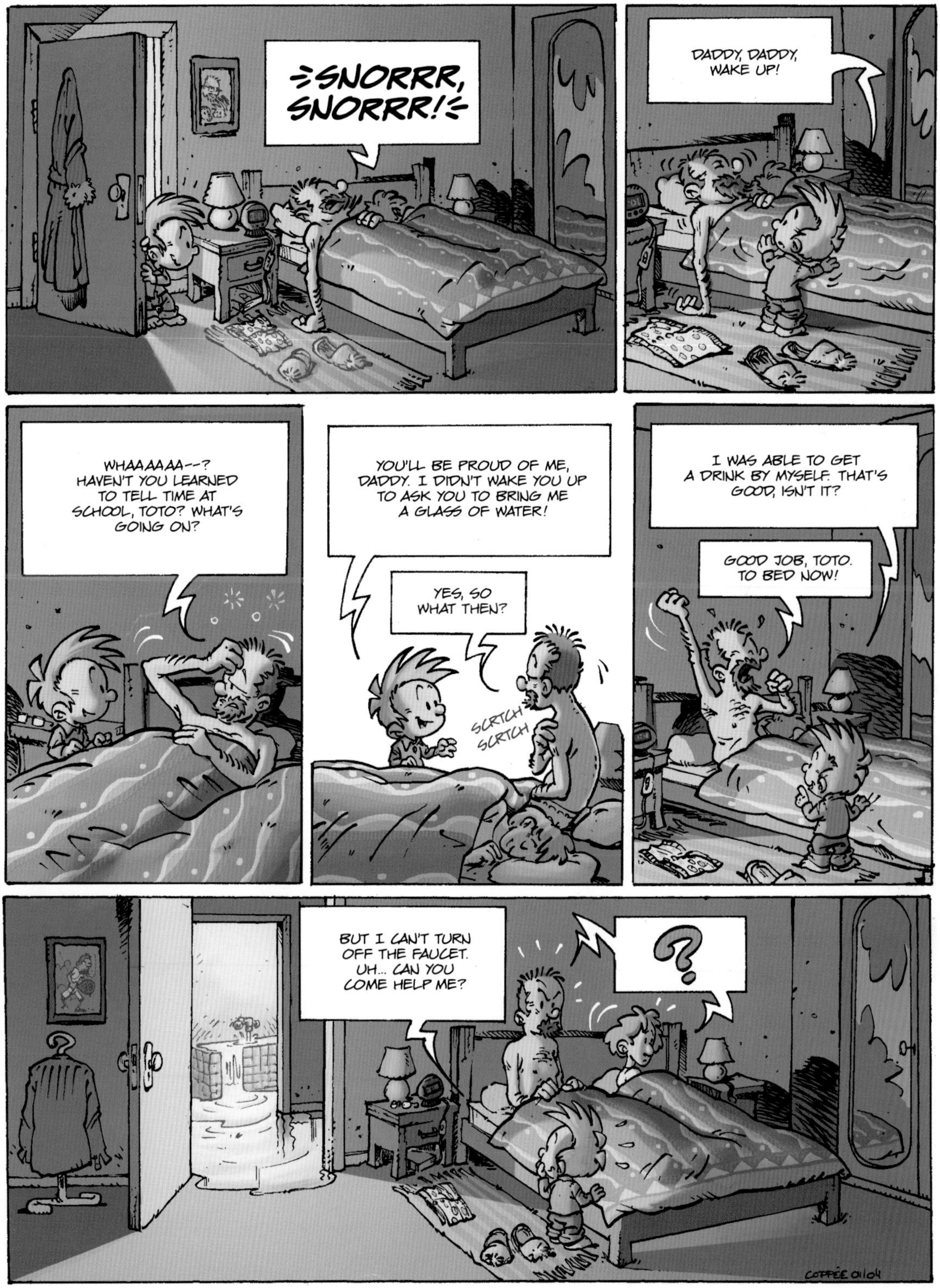

SNORRR, SNORRR!
DADDY, DADDY, WAKE UP!
WHAAAAAA--? HAVEN'T YOU LEARNED TO TELL TIME AT SCHOOL, TOTO? WHAT'S GOING ON?
YOU'LL BE PROUD OF ME, DADDY. I DIDN'T WAKE YOU UP TO ASK YOU TO BRING ME A GLASS OF WATER!
YES, SO WHAT THEN?
SCRTCH SCRTCH
I WAS ABLE TO GET A DRINK BY MYSELF. THAT'S GOOD, ISN'T IT?
GOOD JOB, TOTO. TO BED NOW!
BUT I CAN'T TURN OFF THE FAUCET. UH... CAN YOU COME HELP ME?
?
COPPÉE 01/04

"Service Charges"

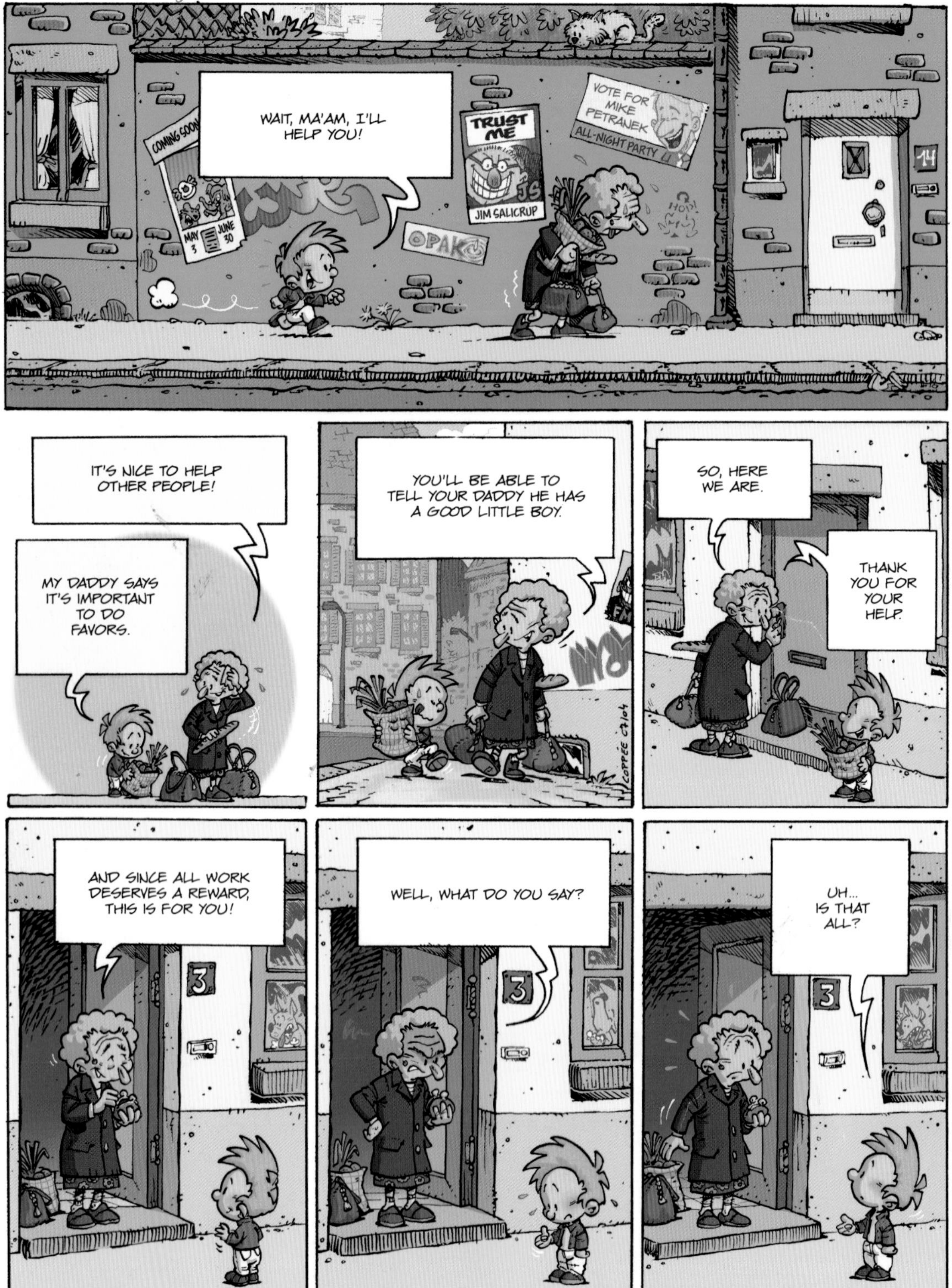

WAIT, MA'AM, I'LL HELP YOU!
COMING SOON
MAY 3
JUNE 30
TRUST ME
JS
JIM SALICRUP
VOTE FOR MIKE PETRANEK
ALL-NIGHT PARTY
OPAK
14
IT'S NICE TO HELP OTHER PEOPLE!
MY DADDY SAYS IT'S IMPORTANT TO DO FAVORS.
YOU'LL BE ABLE TO TELL YOUR DADDY HE HAS A GOOD LITTLE BOY.
COPPÉE 02/04
SO, HERE WE ARE.
THANK YOU FOR YOUR HELP.
AND SINCE ALL WORK DESERVES A REWARD, THIS IS FOR YOU!
3
WELL, WHAT DO YOU SAY?
UH... IS THAT ALL?

"It's All the Same"

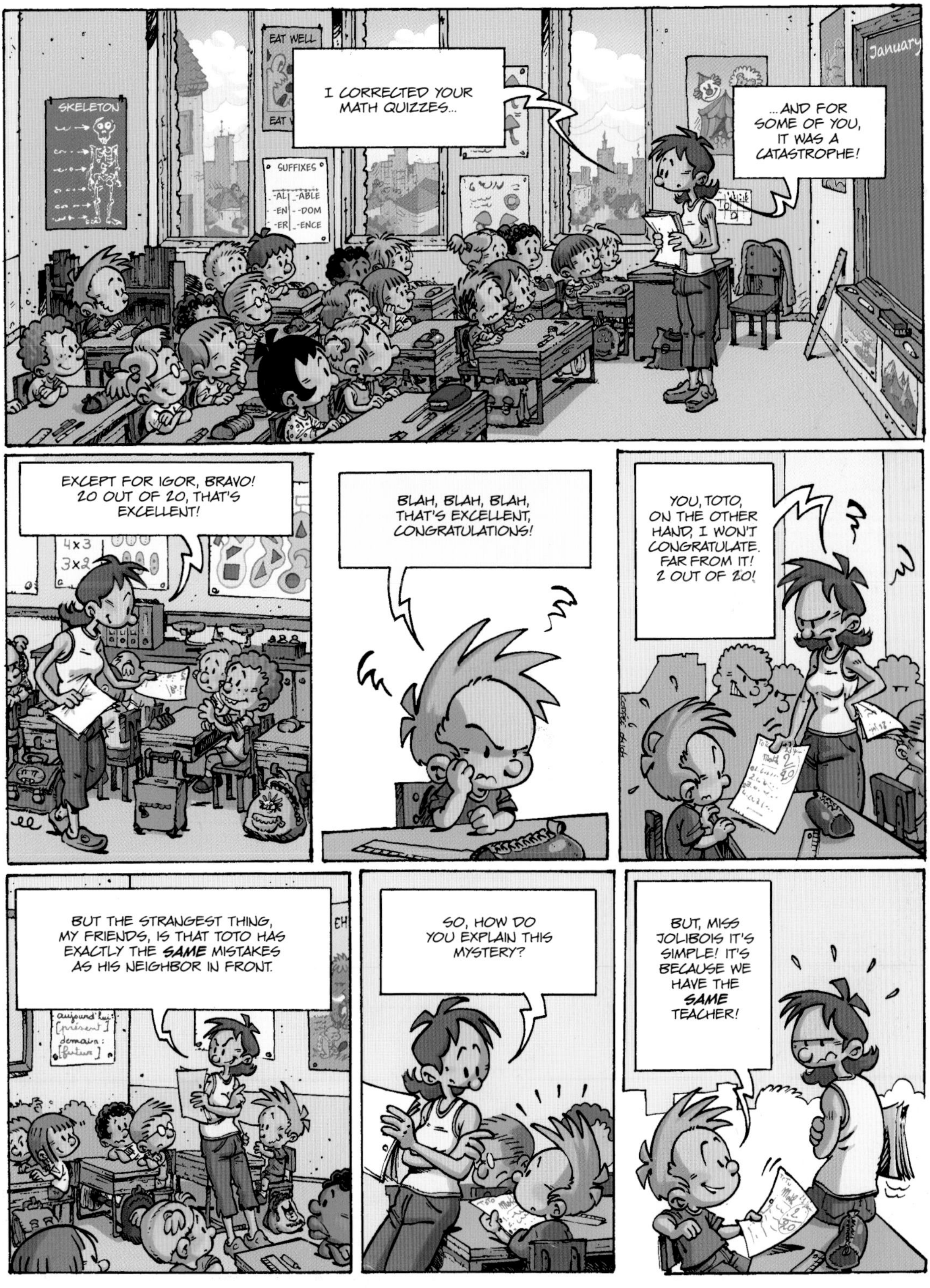

EAT WELL
SKELETON
SUFFIXES
-AL -ABLE
-EN -DOM
-ER -ENCE
January
I CORRECTED YOUR MATH QUIZZES...
...AND FOR SOME OF YOU, IT WAS A CATASTROPHE!
EXCEPT FOR IGOR, BRAVO! 20 OUT OF 20, THAT'S EXCELLENT!
BLAH, BLAH, BLAH, THAT'S EXCELLENT, CONGRATULATIONS!
YOU, TOTO, ON THE OTHER HAND, I WON'T CONGRATULATE. FAR FROM IT! 2 OUT OF 20!
BUT THE STRANGEST THING, MY FRIENDS, IS THAT TOTO HAS EXACTLY THE SAME MISTAKES AS HIS NEIGHBOR IN FRONT.
SO, HOW DO YOU EXPLAIN THIS MYSTERY?
BUT, MISS JOLIBOIS IT'S SIMPLE! IT'S BECAUSE WE HAVE THE SAME TEACHER!

"The Anxiety of the Blank Page"

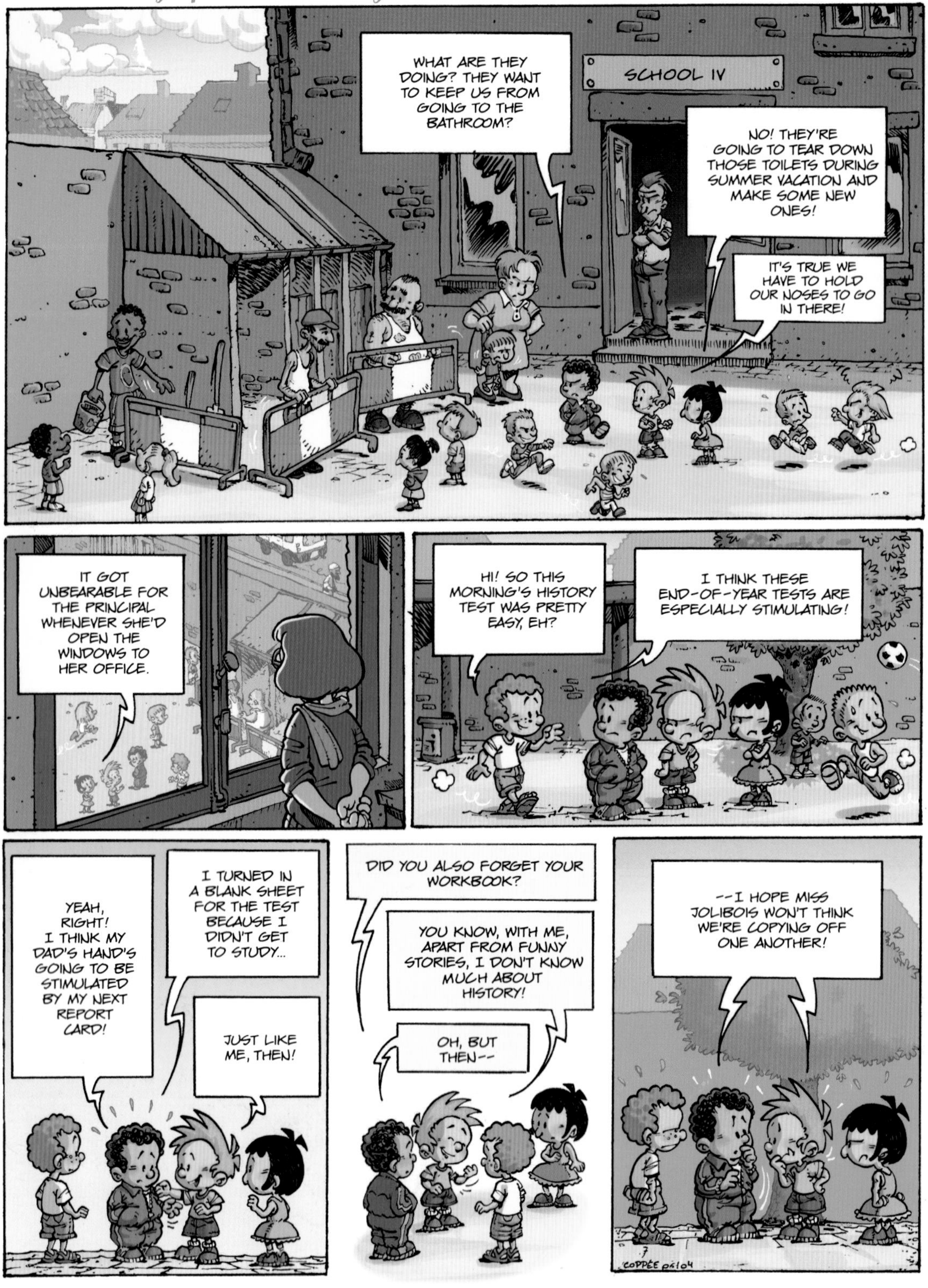
SCHOOL IV
WHAT ARE THEY DOING? THEY WANT TO KEEP US FROM GOING TO THE BATHROOM?
NO! THEY'RE GOING TO TEAR DOWN THOSE TOILETS DURING SUMMER VACATION AND MAKE SOME NEW ONES!
IT'S TRUE WE HAVE TO HOLD OUR NOSES TO GO IN THERE!
IT GOT UNBEARABLE FOR THE PRINCIPAL WHENEVER SHE'D OPEN THE WINDOWS TO HER OFFICE.
HI! SO THIS MORNING'S HISTORY TEST WAS PRETTY EASY, EH?
I THINK THESE END-OF-YEAR TESTS ARE ESPECIALLY STIMULATING!
YEAH, RIGHT! I THINK MY DAD'S HAND'S GOING TO BE STIMULATED BY MY NEXT REPORT CARD!
I TURNED IN A BLANK SHEET FOR THE TEST BECAUSE I DIDN'T GET TO STUDY...
JUST LIKE ME, THEN!
DID YOU ALSO FORGET YOUR WORKBOOK?
YOU KNOW, WITH ME, APART FROM FUNNY STORIES, I DON'T KNOW MUCH ABOUT HISTORY!
OH, BUT THEN--
--I HOPE MISS JOLIBOIS WON'T THINK WE'RE COPYING OFF ONE ANOTHER!
COPPÉE

"A Good Deal"

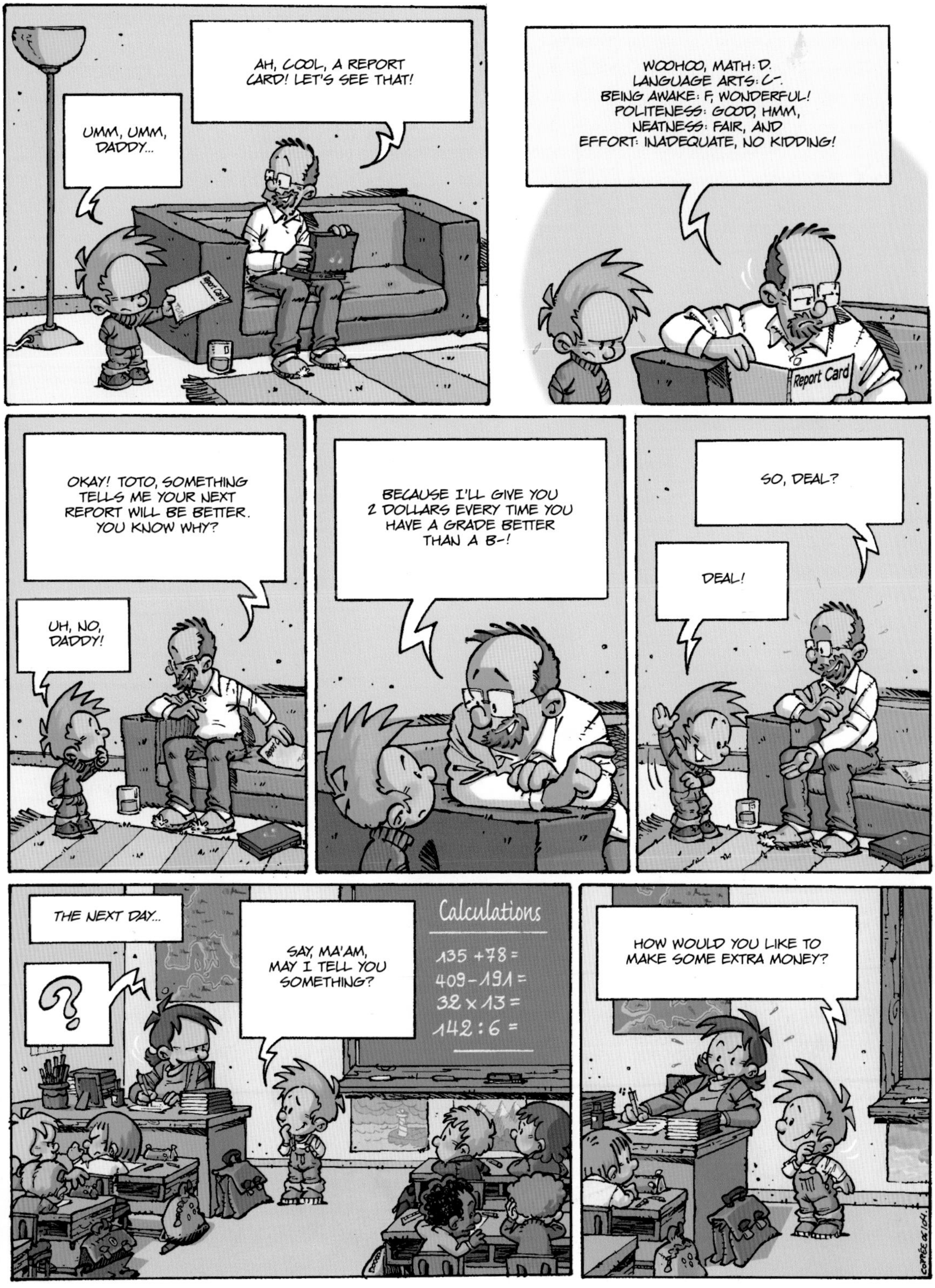
UMM, UMM, DADDY...
AH, COOL, A REPORT CARD! LET'S SEE THAT!
Report Card
WOOHOO, MATH: D. LANGUAGE ARTS: C-. BEING AWAKE: F, WONDERFUL! POLITENESS: GOOD, HMM, NEATNESS: FAIR, AND EFFORT: INADEQUATE, NO KIDDING!
Report Card
OKAY! TOTO, SOMETHING TELLS ME YOUR NEXT REPORT WILL BE BETTER. YOU KNOW WHY?
UH, NO, DADDY!
BECAUSE I'LL GIVE YOU 2 DOLLARS EVERY TIME YOU HAVE A GRADE BETTER THAN A B-!
SO, DEAL?
DEAL!
THE NEXT DAY...
?
SAY, MA'AM, MAY I TELL YOU SOMETHING?
Calculations
135 + 78 =
409 - 191 =
32 x 13 =
142 : 6 =
HOW WOULD YOU LIKE TO MAKE SOME EXTRA MONEY?

"A Very Good Boy"

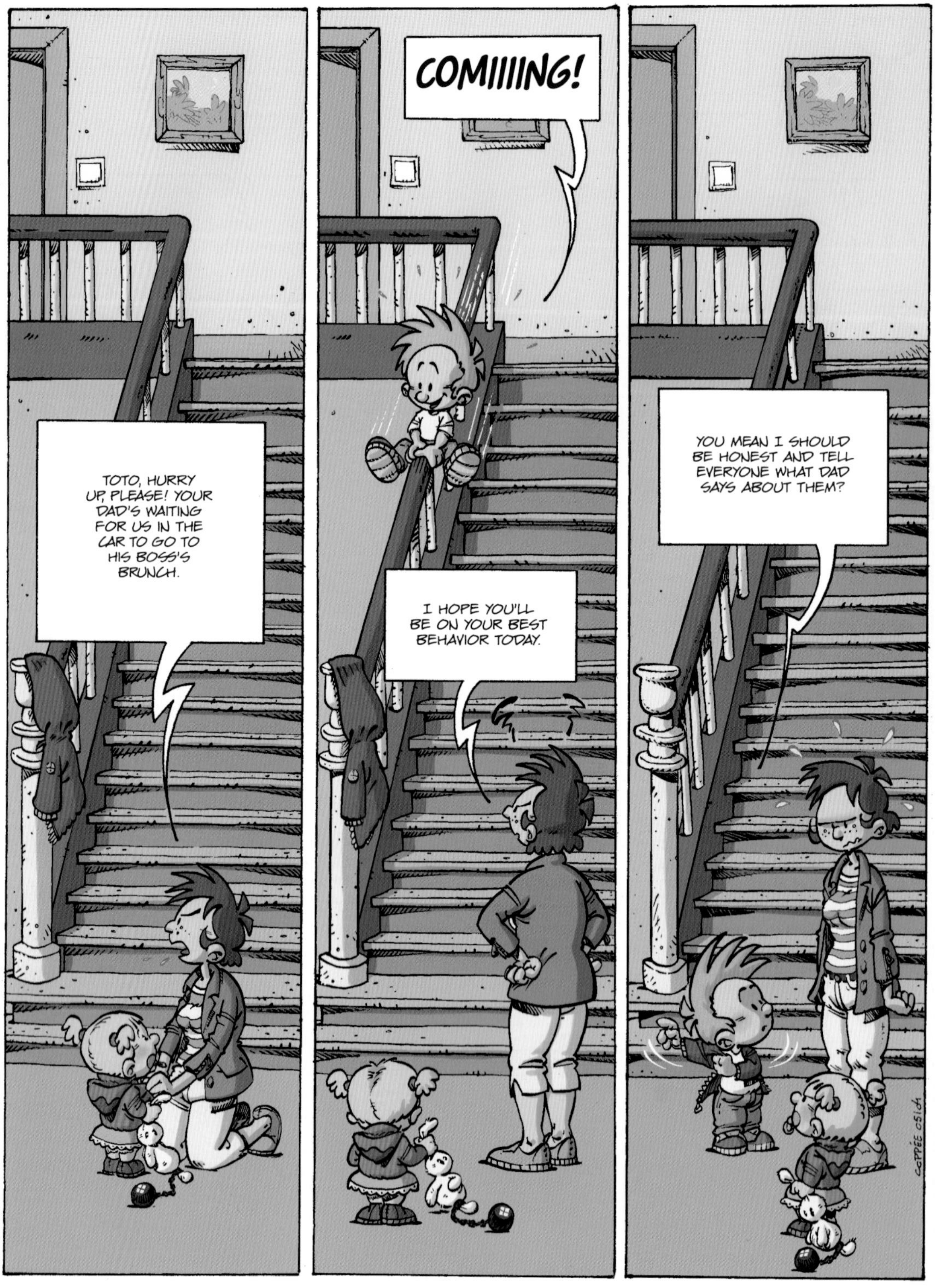
TOTO, HURRY UP, PLEASE! YOUR DAD'S WAITING FOR US IN THE CAR TO GO TO HIS BOSS'S BRUNCH.
COMIIIING!
I HOPE YOU'LL BE ON YOUR BEST BEHAVIOR TODAY.
YOU MEAN I SHOULD BE HONEST AND TELL EVERYONE WHAT DAD SAYS ABOUT THEM?
COPPÉE 05104

"Summer Games"

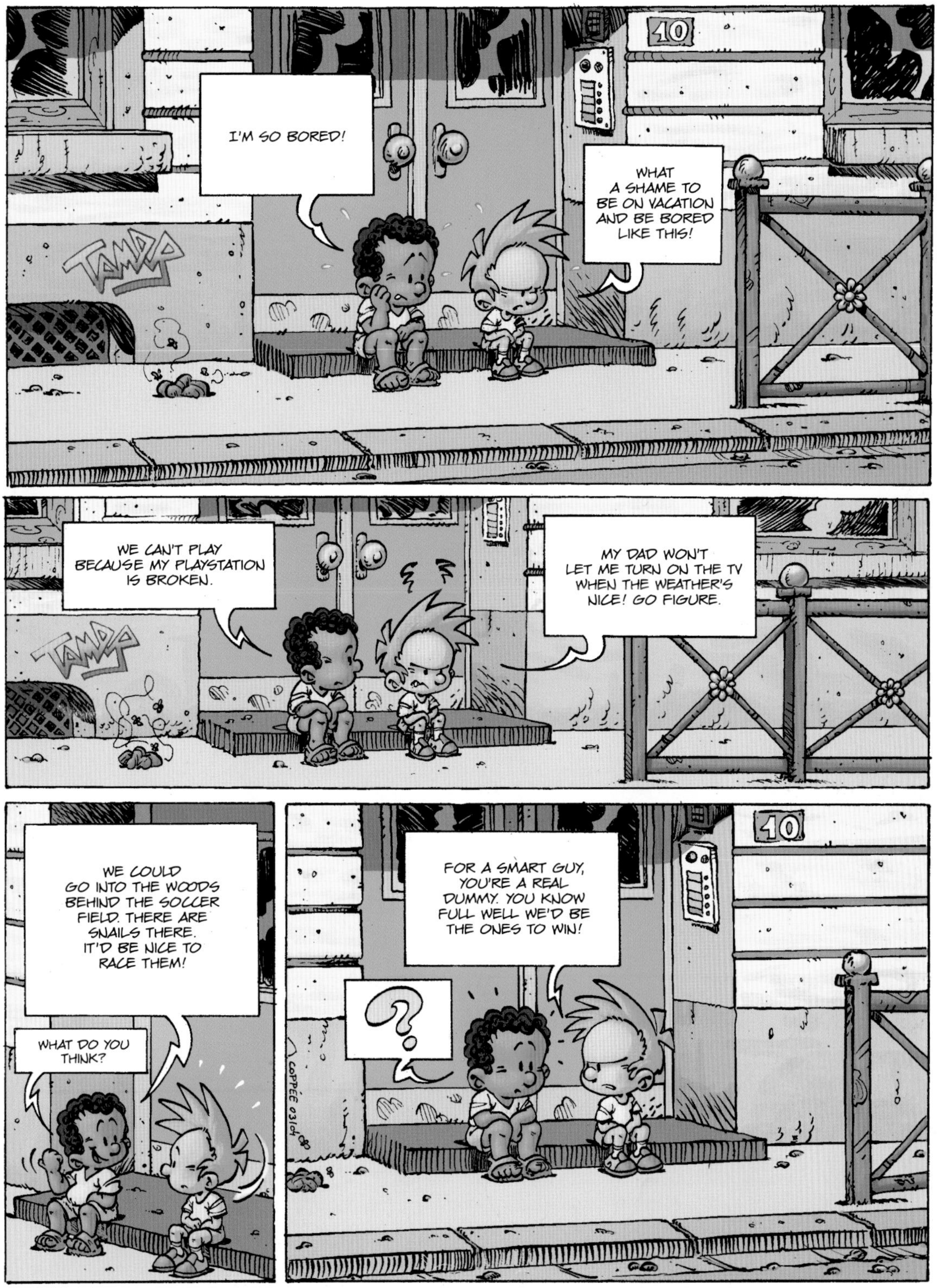
I'M SO BORED!
WHAT A SHAME TO BE ON VACATION AND BE BORED LIKE THIS!
WE CAN'T PLAY BECAUSE MY PLAYSTATION IS BROKEN.
MY DAD WON'T LET ME TURN ON THE TV WHEN THE WEATHER'S NICE! GO FIGURE.
WE COULD GO INTO THE WOODS BEHIND THE SOCCER FIELD. THERE ARE SNAILS THERE. IT'D BE NICE TO RACE THEM!
WHAT DO YOU THINK?
FOR A SMART GUY, YOU'RE A REAL DUMMY. YOU KNOW FULL WELL WE'D BE THE ONES TO WIN!
?
COPPÉE 03/04

"Observation Skills"

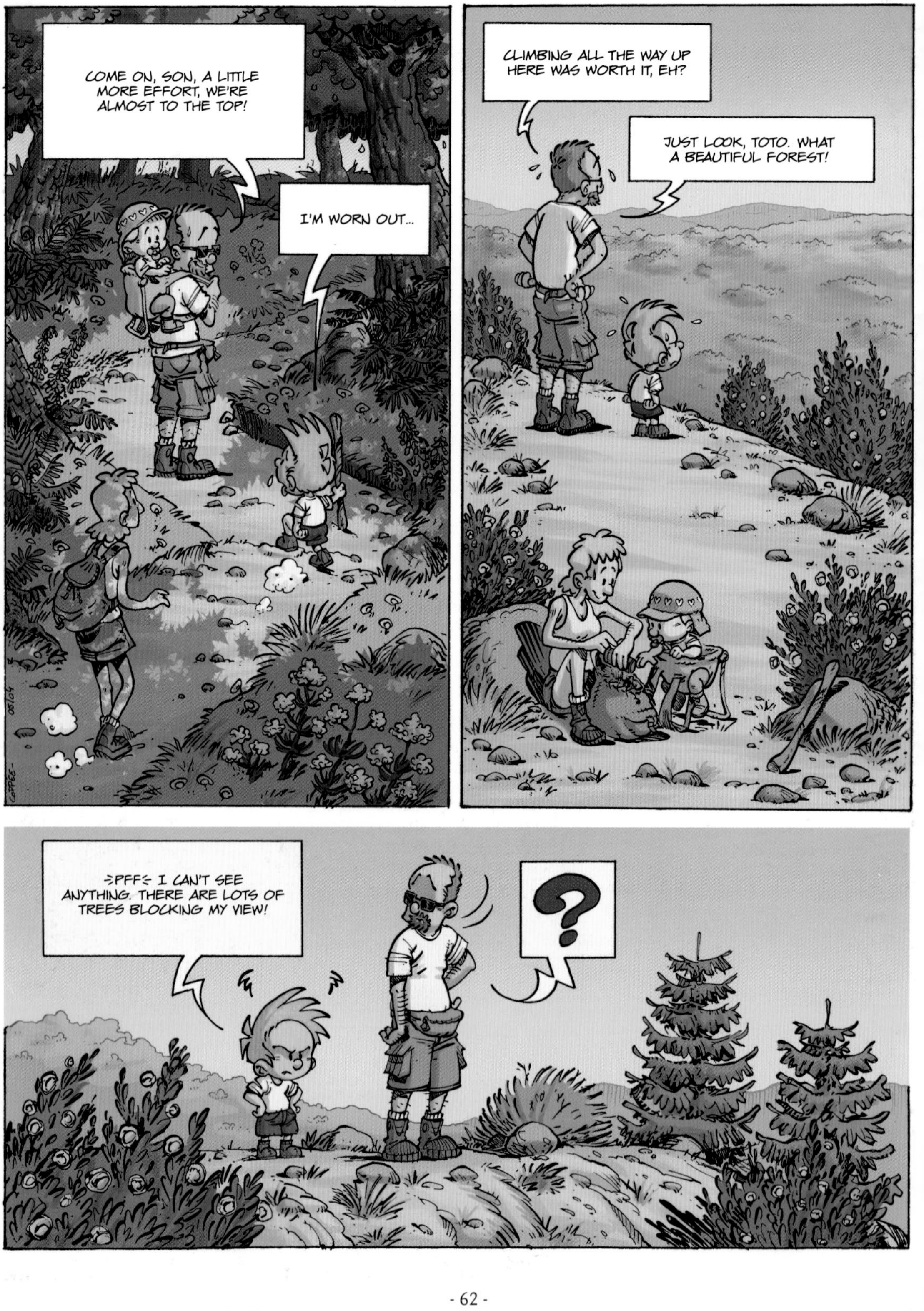

COME ON, SON, A LITTLE MORE EFFORT, WE'RE ALMOST TO THE TOP!
I'M WORN OUT...
CLIMBING ALL THE WAY UP HERE WAS WORTH IT, EH?
JUST LOOK, TOTO. WHAT A BEAUTIFUL FOREST!
=PFF= I CAN'T SEE ANYTHING. THERE ARE LOTS OF TREES BLOCKING MY VIEW!
?

WATCH OUT FOR PAPERCUTZ

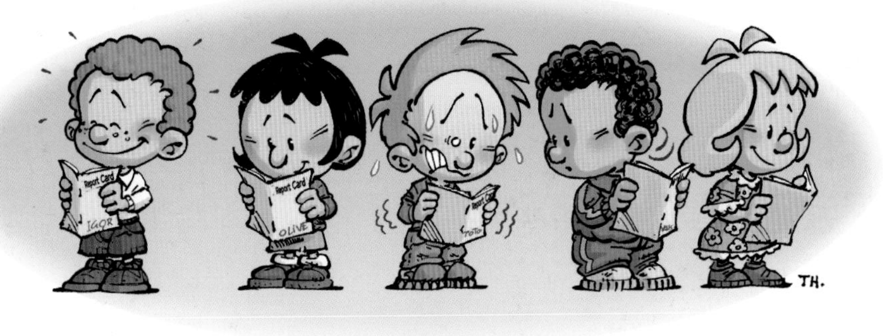
Report Card
IGOR
Report Card
OLIVE
TOTO
TH.

Welcome to the fun-filled, formerly-French, first TOTO TROUBLE graphic novel by Thierry Coppée from Papercutz, the petite comics company dedicated to publishing great graphic novels for all ages. I'm Jim Salicrup, the Editor-in-Chief at Papercutz and substitute teacher at Toto's school.

We're thrilled to add TOTO TROUBLE to our ever-expanding line-up of graphic novels. We're big fans of little Toto, and we hope you enjoy his jokes as much as we do. In fact, this series was originally published in France and called "*Les Blagues de Toto*," which is "Toto's Jokes." We changed the name of the series to TOTO TROUBLE to tie-in to the animated series featuring Toto that ran on the Starz channel, but if you blinked, you probably missed it.

Fortunately, you didn't need to watch the TV show, to enjoy TOTO TROUBLE. In fact, to even further enhance your enjoyment of TOTO TROUBLE we've come up with a scorecard (Bet you thought we were kidding on the back cover!) for you to keep track of the jokes in this occasionally gross and goofy graphic novel. Now it gets a little tricky sometimes—believe me, I've tried it—but the goal here is to use Roman numerals to keep track of how many of the various type of jokes are in this volume.

Dad Jokes	
Dead Cat Jokes	
Dead Dog Jokes	
Dead Goldfish Jokes	
Dumb Student Jokes	
Eating-a-Slug Jokes	
Poop (No Joke, Just Poop)	
Poop Jokes	
Teacher Jokes	
Toto-is-Dumb Jokes	
Tricking-Mom Jokes	
Tricking School Jokes	
Wee-Wee Jokes	

You may have noticed on some pages, five to be precise, various people are awarded prizes for jokes. These are the winning entries in a joke competition held in France, where amongst the prizes, the winning jokes got to be published in *Les Blagues de Toto* and illustrated by Thierry Coppée himself (We'll have a photo and bio of Toto's creator in TOTO TROUBLE #2!) What do you think of having a joke competition like that here in TOTO TROUBLE? Let us know by contacting us by the various means listed below. You can also tell us what you thought of TOTO TROUBLE #1 "Back to Crass." If you liked it, feel free to post or tweet about TOTO TROUBLE online. And don't forget to look for TOTO TROUBLE #2 "A Deadly Jokester" coming soon to the bookstore nearest you!

So until next time, be sure to stay out of trouble!

Thanks,

Jim

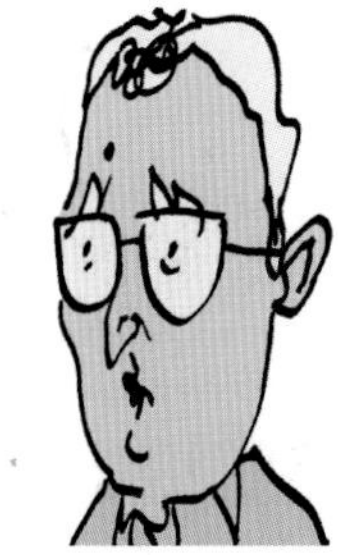

STAY IN TOUCH!

EMAIL: salicrup@papercutz.com
WEB: papercutz.com
TWITTER: @papercutzgn
FACEBOOK: PAPERCUTZGRAPHICNOVELS
MAIL: Papercutz, 160 Broadway, Suite 700, East Wing, New York, NY 10038

More Great Graphic Novels from PAPERCUTZ

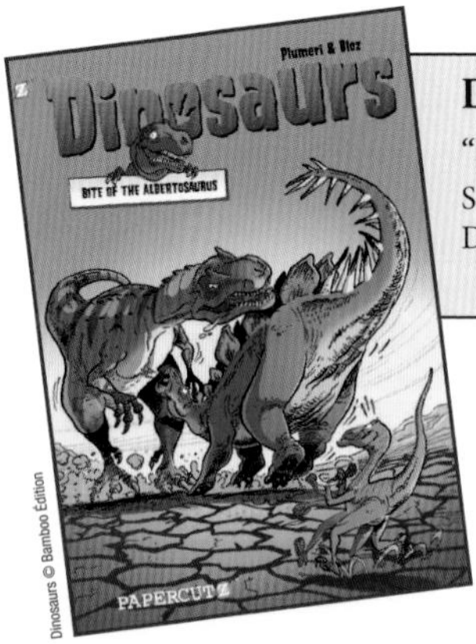

Plumeri & Bloz
Dinosaurs
BITE OF THE ALBERTOSAURUS
PAPERCUTZ

DINOSAURS #2
"Bite of the Albertosaurus"
Science facts combined with Dino-humor!

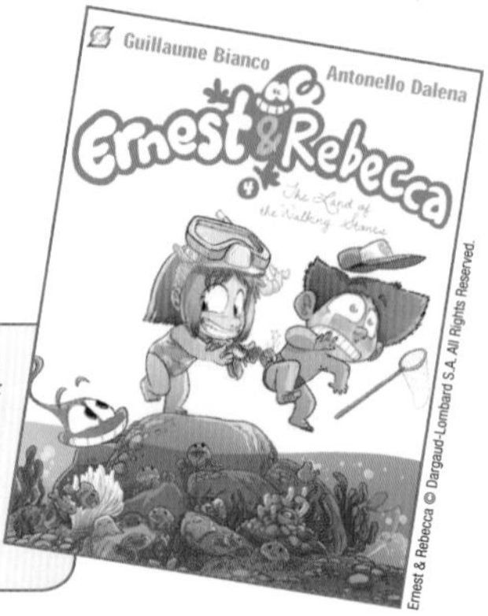

Guillaume Bianco
Antonello Dalena
Ernest & Rebecca

ERNEST & REBECCA #4
"The Land of Walking Stones"
A 6 ½ year old girl and her micro-bial buddy against the world!

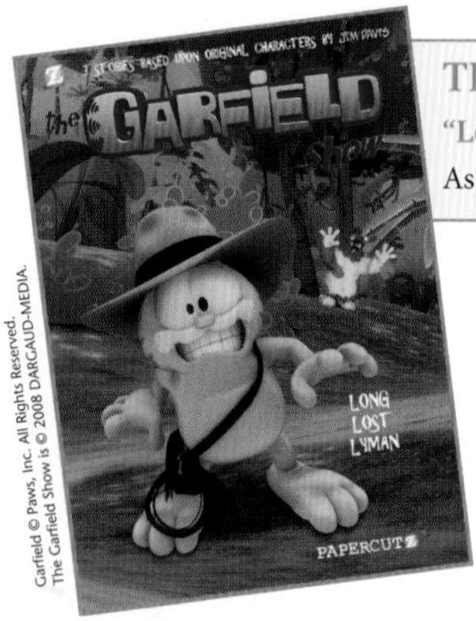

7 STORIES BASED UPON ORIGINAL CHARACTERS BY JIM DAVIS
the GARFIELD Show
LONG LOST LYMAN
PAPERCUTZ

THE GARFIELD SHOW #3
"Long Lost Lyman"
As seen on the Cartoon Network!

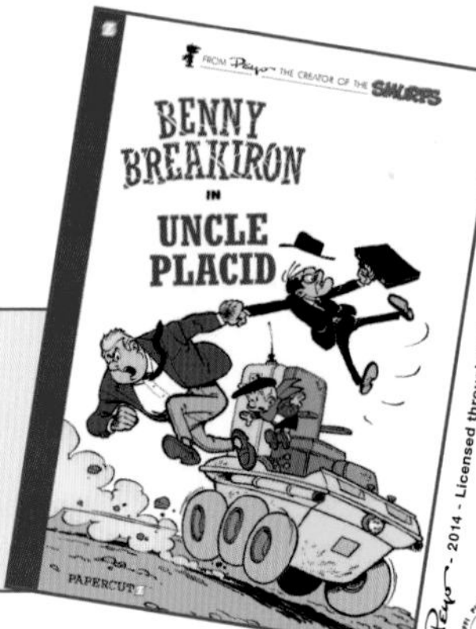

BENNY BREAKIRON
IN
UNCLE PLACID
PAPERCUTZ

BENNY BREAKIRON #4
"Uncle Placid"
Benny helps his Uncle protect the finance minister of Fürengrootsbadenschtein from all kinds of dangerous danger!

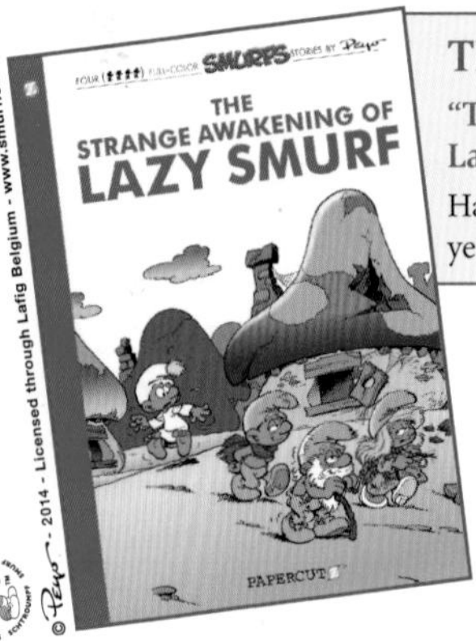

SMURFS
THE STRANGE AWAKENING OF LAZY SMURF
PAPERCUTZ

THE SMURFS #17
"The Strange Awakening of Lazy Smurf"
Has Lazy Smurf been asleep for 200 years?

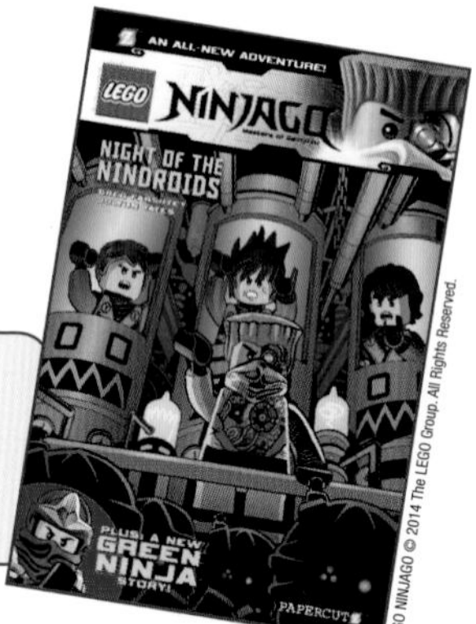

AN ALL-NEW ADVENTURE!
LEGO NINJAGO
NIGHT OF THE NINDROIDS
PLUS: A NEW GREEN NINJA STORY!
PAPERCUTZ

LEGO® NINJAGO #9
"Night of the Nindroids"
Will Zane betray his friends? Plus, an all-new Green Ninja Story!

Available at better booksellers everywhere!

Or order directly from us! DINOSAURS is available in hardcover only for $10.99; ERNEST & REBECCA is $11.99 in hardcover only; THE GARFIELD SHOW is available in paperback for $7.99, in hardcover for $11.99; BENNY BREAKIRON is available in hardcover only for $11.99; THE SMURFS are available in paperback for $5.99, in hardcover for $10.99; and LEGO NINJAGO is available in paperback for $6.99 and hardcover for $10.99.

Please add $4.00 for postage and handling for the first book, add $1.00 for each additional book.

Please make check payable to NBM Publishing. Send to: PAPERCUTZ, 160 Broadway, Suite 700, East Wing, New York, NY 10038 (1-800-886-1223)